THE AUSSIE CRUSADERS

THE
AUSSIE CRUSADERS

WITH ALLENBY IN PALESTINE

By
JOSEPH BOWES

Illustrated by
WAL PAGET

LIVING BOOK PRESS

2017

This edition published 2017
By Living Book Press
147 Durren Rd, Jilliby, 2259
Copyright © Living Book Press, 2017

Cover Painting by George Lambert

National Library of Australia's Cataloguing-in-Publication entry:

Creator: Bowes, Joseph, author.
Title: The Aussie crusaders with Allenby in Palestine / Jospeh
                        Bowes ; illustrated by Wal Paget.
ISBN: 9780648035671 (paperback)
Target Audience: For primary school age.
Subjects: Australia. Army. Australian Light Horse.--Juvenile fiction.
                    Australia. Army. Australian and New Zealand Army
Corps.   --Juvenile fiction.
                    World War, 1914-1918--Juvenile fiction.
Other Creators/
Contributors: Paget, Walter, 1863-1935, illustrator.

HARP of Memnon! sweetly strung
    To the music of the spheres;
While the hero's dirge is sung,
    Breathe enchantment to our ears.
Let thy numbers, soft and slow,
    O'er the plain with carnage spread,
Soothe the dying while they flow
    To the memory of the dead.
Then thy tones triumphant pour,
    Let them pierce the hero's grave;
Life's tumultuous battle o'er,
    O, how sweetly sleep the brave!
From the dust their laurels bloom,
    High they shoot and flourish free;
Glory's temple is the tomb;
    Death is immortality.

-JAMES MONTGOMERY.

Contents

CHAPTER I

HOW THE AUSSIES FELL INTO THE HANDS OF THE BEDOUINS

"ARE you awake, Major?"

"Ssshh!"

The low tones of the speaker, at this sibilant warning, fined down to the barest whisper. Could they have been seen in the enveloping darkness, the persons between whom a whispered dialogue proceeded would have been identified by their uniforms as British soldiers. They were both young men, the younger of the two being little more than a lad. The other was older by some years. The elder was built on a large scale. His frame had height and breadth, but was somewhat lacking in depth, for he was "slab-chested," and did not carry an ounce of superfluous flesh. But for all that his bones were well covered with masses of muscle and sinew which betokened greater strength and hardihood than would have been suggested by an ampler proportion of flesh and fat. His youthful comrade was undoubtedly a greater favourite of nature. In height and looks he stood in contrast to his companion. Whereas the elder lacked symmetry, the younger was well formed. His handsome yet strong face, broad shoulders, narrow hips, and muscular limbs denoted a combination of body and mind to be seriously reckoned with in any contest either of limb or will. He would be no quitter in any undertaking to which he bent his energies.

The darkness is rapidly dissolving before the advancing dawn, and the twittering birds in the overhead branches proclaim the advent of a new day. The dim outlines of prone figures now become distinct. The soldiers are not free agents. They lie on the earth, tightly bound; while around them are closely grouped a number of picturesque villains clad in Eastern raiment. One glance at them is sufficient to indicate their type: they are Bedouins. These fellows, about a score in number, thus surrounding their captives, have passed the night in a small oasis. In the first flush of dawn they bestir themselves, and are soon consuming their frugal breakfast, heedless of the hunger and thirst of the prisoners.

While the Bedouins are discussing their scanty meal, let us take a closer view of their victims. While tightly bound they are not gagged, a merciful exemption, and hardly to be expected from villains of the type of their present masters. Judging from their dishevelled appearance they have received a rough handling. Their uniforms are as far from being spick and span as one could well conceive. Their tunics are buttonless: the congenital thieves have seen to that. Their clothes are not only soiled with the accumulated dirt of months, but indelibly stained with blotches of blood which have faded to the colour of a rusty-brown. Their dust-begrimed features are hard-drawn, as though they had passed through a prolonged physical and mental strain which had fixed its character in their faces. Yet for all their dirt, untidiness, body-weariness, and haggard looks, one fails to find any sign of depression about them. There is no such torpor or apathy as fatalism breeds, nor any down-in-the-mouth bearing as a consequence of their extreme hardships and present parlous condition.

The only thing which appears to give them any concern at present is the prospect of food and drink. Otherwise their bearing, as far as can be judged—with the obvious restrictions of their bound limbs—if not defiant, is certainly that of "No surrender." Body and brain are worn —if marks go for anything—almost to breaking-point, yet the strapped limbs, tensely-drawn features, most of all their bloodshot eyes, are still obedient to their light-hearted spirits.

"Did you get any sleep, Major?"

"As much as the cords and your snores permitted."

"What? *Me*, snore?"

"Yes, you, you poor innocent. Had to prod you several times. The very camels stopped snarling and listened with astonishment and envy to the variety of your notes."

"Garn! You will have your joke, Mister Jack."

"Well, a joke's a long way better than nothing, and that's about all we can count upon from this bunch, Judging from appearances. The beggars are wrapping up the little that's left. How long is it, Jock, since we pulped any food?"

"We've swallered nothin' but powder-smoke an' desert-dust since afore daylight yesterday, barrin', o'course, the contents of our waterbottles."

"True; and the water gave out before midday—at least mine did. Suppose we remind these absent-minded beggars that a swig of well-water and a few crumbs of their unconsumed tucker would not have to be offered more than once?"

Suiting the action to a word, he sang out as lustily as his parched mouth allowed to the men who were now at their camels, preparing for an immediate start.

"Hi, Abdul! Come here! D'y'hear?"

To give effect to his words the younger man, who had been addressed by his companion as Major, wriggled into a sitting position. He addressed the men in Arabic, using the name "Abdul" in the same way that we call every Chinaman "John." It was not until he had called repeatedly that one of the number deigned to come. But to all requests for food and drink he turned a deaf ear. After bestowing several choice expletives upon the captives, he left them, returning to the group of men who were now ready for the march. It became quite evident to the unfortunate soldiers that they were to be treated as a wholly negligible quantity. The tortures of hunger and thirst, instead of exciting the compassion of their captors, produced contrary feeling. The more the prisoners suffered the greater was their pleasure.

Notwithstanding their fortitude, this callous treatment produced strong feelings in the breasts of the captives. Could words have injured them, these desert aborigines would have had a short shrift. Words, however, break no bones, though they act as a safety-valve to the utterer.

"Might as well save our breath," said the youthful officer to his comrade, who wore a sergeant's chevrons. "Here come two of the beggars to haul us to the camels. They're going to pitch us across the saddles as though we were bundles of hay, and rope us for security. Not a very pleasant picnic before us, eh? Wonder to me they haven't slit our throats. That pleasantry may come later. Anyway, while there's life there's hope. Are we down-hearted?"

The "N—o—o" which came in response to the challenge, if not so cordial in tone as it would have been upon an ordinary occasion, was indicative of the spirit which inspired the young men under the heavy trials to which they were being subjected.

To their great relief, however, the first act of the natives was to cut the thongs which bound their limbs.

"Good enough!" cried the major, as he flung his arms about and stamped his feet to induce circulation. "I'll take back some of the nasty things I said about the beggars."

"If they'll follow this with giving us a good square drink I'll be willing to wipe the slate clean of all ill names."

This conditional promise was fulfilled a few minutes later. When the prisoners had been brought along to the camels, their physical distress became so evident to their captors that, through no spirit of compunction, or pity, but rather from mercenary motives, the sheikh, after a momentary hesitation, ordered their guards to take them to the well near by, where they were quickly doing their best to drain it of the brackish water that it produced. That they did not succeed in so doing must be laid to the sheikh, whose peremptory command to mount was followed by their being dragged from the well and ordered to bestride a camel which had been reserved for them.

The disadvantages of "double-banking" were countervailed by the opportunities that were thus given them to converse. After they had mounted, their arms were tied to the saddle to prevent escape, but their legs were left free.

This was much better than they had hoped for. The comparative freedom of their limbs together with the copious draught of well-water, when compared with their cramped and painful experience of the past night, produced a pleasant sense of exhilaration.

"What made the old general change his mind all of a sudden an' give us a drink, Major?"

"Let us call it humanity, Jock."

"Humanity be blowed! I was watching the old rascal. There's not a spark of humanity in him."

"I'll admit that appearances are against him; but, like the Queensland nut which has a shell of flint to cover the sweetest of kernels, so—"

"So far as that old villain is concerned, I give you my word for it, he's all shell and no kernel at all. Why, when he told his men to take us to the well his eyes were glinting all the time. There's no lovemakin' in this business, you may take your oath on that."

"Well, Sergeant, perhaps you can give the reasons yourself."

"Well, the old rascal, in my opinion, saw that if he didn't give us some little attention he stood to lose by us. It's like a drover who takes along a mob of fats for the market. He'll see to it that the beasts don't die before he delivers 'em, not through any feeling of humanity, but from self-interest. So this dago does without askin' what all your appealin' failed to get, simply because he sees there's a chance of losing the goods unless he looks after 'em a bit."

"Meaning he's going to hold us to ransom, and that his apparent humanity, after all, is only cupidity? Well, I believe you're right. The old chap's on the make. He doesn't want us to die on his hands, anyway."

"It's a rotten bit of bad luck, isn't it, sir, to be taken like this at the heel of the hunt, after we'd given the jolly Jackoes such a father of a licking? To be taken while you were lying insensible, an' I was tryin' to rouse you! At that very moment, who should appear but this lot of scum, and had me on the broad of my back afore I could say Jack Robinson."

"It's bad enough, old fellow, but it might have been much worse. We're alive, and our limbs are still attached to our bodies, and that's more than you can say for hundreds of our mates."

"Right you are, sir! We're alive and kickin'."

"Don't know so much about the kicking, Jock," replied the major, with a smile. "The last two days took pretty well every ounce of energy out of me. What with the all-night marching and the fighting from dawn to dark, and then being hustled the first half of last night, bound to the back of a draught-camel, doesn't find one in the best fettle for entering a high-kicking contest for the championship."

"No, sir, it don't; but if I was on the ground an' the ole boss of this tribe stood wid his back towards me, bent forward a bit, I'm game to wager I'd lift him in the air a few yards."

"If I were a betting man, M'Thirst, I'm certain I wouldn't bet on the chance, for I'm sure you'd win," said the officer with a hearty laugh.

"Here, old fellow," said he a little later, after fumbling in the breast-pocket of his tunic. "If I cannot aid you in carrying out that attractive programme of revenge, I can help you to the enjoyment of the next best thing. Here's a cig."

"A fag, sir? Good Christopher! Why, it's a thousand years since I had one in my lips."

CHAPTER II

HOW THE PRISONERS FARED ON THE WAY

WHEN the Bedouins broke camp they followed a northerly course, which led them through broken country. High, rocky ridges with intervening declivities surrounded them. As they advanced through this maze they passed patches of green sward, with here and there clusters of wild flowers of brilliant hue. At intervals were stone walls in a dilapidated condition. They also passed some rudely constructed cairns which doubtless, long ago, had been shelters and storehouses. Here also were stone dwellings in a ruinous condition. In addition there were many signs of ancient cultivation. This all pointed to a time when the deserted country sustained a population of farmers, who, with hard toil, won a scanty living from the fertile patches along the wadies. It pointed, in fact, to a time anterior to Arab occupation; for even new-chums, like the two prisoners perched upon the camel's back, would never have associated the ruins of walls, houses, dams, and cairns with the shiftless, lazy nomads of whom their captors were a type. Everything pointed to a thrifty, industrious class who one time won a living by patient endeavour, while on the other hand the present neglected and deserted condition amply justified the common saying that everything goes to ruin in an Arab's hands.

Despite their weariness, the two young men were greatly interested in the character of the country through which they were passing.

"Keep your eyes skinned, Jock. It may help us later on to remember the route which we are now taking."

Thus the younger of the two, who, in despite of age, was the senior, not only in experience but in authority.

His features and general mien proclaimed a highly-trained intelligence. His eyes were the chief attraction of his face. They were remarkable for depth rather than their size. They held within their keeping all seen things. Not a detail escaped them. Every phase of the landscape was photographed and fixed in his brain by the perfect lenses of his eyes, as they journeyed along the tortuous track. Should the information thus acquired ever be wanted he could draw it from his mental storehouse as easily as unwinding ribbon from a reel.

Major Jack Smith had been one of a band of young Australians who had followed the occupation of kangaroo hunters, making a living out of the scalps and pelts. Being youths of spirit and wit they had humorously christened themselves "The Eureka Amalgamateds." When war broke out and the call to arms was sounded throughout Australia, these young Queenslanders were among the first to enlist, and had the honour of being included in the First Expeditionary Force. They were drafted into the Light Horse, where they early made the acquaintance of Jock M'Thirst, a product of the civilisation of the Far West. Jack had a strong influence over Mac in the first stages of training. The influence was wholly for good, for M'Thirst broke away from certain habits that, without doubt, were detrimental to his character. Smith and his companions did their bit in Gallipoli, winning stripes, honours, and wounds.

After the evacuation they did their full share in the desert campaign, by which, after many months of hardships and any amount of tough fighting, the Turks were driven northward from the Suez Canal to the borders of Palestine. Their last stronghold in the Sinai Peninsula, the well-fortified town of Rafa, had, on the day before the opening of this story, been assaulted by the British, and after a stiff, all-day fight had been captured by desperate assault, and before large bodies of Turks, who were hastening from the Beersheba base to the help of the beleaguered garrison, could effect a junction. It was while pursuing these same reinforcements, after breaking the head of the column, that Jack Smith and Jock M'Thirst were unfortunate enough to be unhorsed in a melee during a partial rally of the fleeing Turks. Neither of the two men was missed by their comrades, who swept forward on the heels of the hunt. It was while Jock was attending to Jack, who had been stunned in the fall, that a predatory band of Arabs swooped down on them and captured them.

So far the prisoners were in utter ignorance of what their fate was likely to be. The sheikh had neither questioned them nor caused them to be questioned. Seemingly he took no more interest in them than if they were logs of wood. The only thing to be gathered during the morning's ride was that they had crossed the border and were travelling in a north-easterly direction.

"So this is what they call the Holy Land, Mister Jack," exclaimed M'Thirst, shortly after Jack had told him of his conviction.

"Yes, we're right into Palestine, old man. The most historic bit of country on God's earth."

"It may be all you say, but for all that I'm not taken with it, so far, anyhow. There's nothing to blow about the land. Why, one acre of the Darling Downs would grow more than a hundred of this land. It'd take a hundred acres of this stuff to feed a bandicoot."

"Not quite so bad as that, Sergeant. Still, so far, it's barren soil. It'll improve, I dare say, when we get on a bit. Even now it's a jolly sight better than the everlasting sand-dunes of the desert."

"You are right, Major. But where do you think we're going?"

"Well, that's more than I can answer. Only the Bedouins can reveal that secret. I thought early in the day that they'd be heading for Beersheba, but gave up that long ago, for Beersheba lies almost due east from where we were this morning."

As they continued in the same direction hour after

hour, Jack's growing convictions were confirmed. Far from seeking the great Turkish base, his captors were avoiding it.

There could be no denying that the two youths were keenly interested in their fate. Their feelings were rather those of intense curiosity than of fearful apprehension. Jack was firmly convinced in his mind that no immediate harm threatened them; that beyond the discomforts incidental to prisondom they had nothing to fear; and that these conscienceless vagabonds had appraised their lives as something of value and therefore worth preserving.

The party drew rein about noon in a patch of vegetation which grew round an old well. Rapidly dismounting, they made preparation for feeding and siesta under the shade of an ancient tamarisk tree. Having pursued a course of forced travel for about seven hours, they believed themselves to be well beyond the range of pursuit, should the friends of the prisoners follow up with the thought of rescue. With a sense of safety came a relaxation of vigilance. During the ride they had answered the questionings of their captives with scowls and profanity, refusing a word of information, and at the same time promising all kinds of torture. Now they became mild by comparison. The thongs were removed from their hands, and they were allowed to walk about freely within the limits of the patch of vegetation, too tiny to be dignified by the name of oasis.

Their captors unbent so far as to give civil replies to direct questions. The prisoners gained nothing, however, by civility. The answers were characteristically evasive. The Eastern, as is well known to those having anything to do with him, is a past-master in the art of bluffing. For no reason at all oftentimes that one can see, he will weave a web of artful speech calculated to hide the truth. To call him an inveterate liar, as indeed he seems to be from the Western view-point, is to apply a term that is hardly fair to him. At any rate, the charge would sound less harsh and not so much an impeachment of his virtue, were one to describe it as an innate tendency to obscure the issues. Being a direct descendant of the great Bedouin Patriarch, Ishmael, whose hand was against every man, it is not to be wondered that the Arab has inherited a vast store of desert wisdom in which artful speech finds ample scope.

The prisoners relished the rest and freedom beyond telling. The handful of dried fruit given them scarcely affected the pangs of hunger. But they had been trained in a hard school, and had learned to suffer hunger with the minimum of complaint and a spice of philosophy. For hunger they had the compensation of slaking their thirst at the well with copious supplies of sweet, cool water. Having eaten the dates and drunk to repletion, they lay down on the sward under the grateful shade of the trees and became unconscious immediately to their surroundings. They slept the dreamless sleep of fatigue.

They were roused with difficulty three hours later. The Bedouins were ready for the road. This time their hands were left free, an indication that their masters had little fear of their escape. The rest and sleep had done wonders for them, and as they jogged along in a swinging shuffle at a slower gait than previously, the mercury of their spirits rose steadily. The country, though rough, improved in fertility as they progressed through the late afternoon. The ground rose higher. A watercourse ran along the middle of a wady whose windings they followed for some miles. The banks were covered with a bright green sward. They passed chains of small pools of limpid water in the watercourse. Now and then they pulled up at an old well surrounded by stone troughs, placed there for watering stock.

Wild flowers were an added charm. Many of the varieties were unknown to the Australian lads, but they identified clusters of beautiful irises of varying shades and brilliant patches of scarlet anemones. To the smiling beauty of the lush grass and the flowers—so grateful to eyes that for many weary months had been strained with the merciless glare of desert sands, relieved only by the dull greens of shrubs—were to be added the flitting forms and songs of birds. Thrushes, doves, and other sweet songsters raised a concord of joyous music as the evening advanced. Once when passing through a field of wheat stubble a covey of quail rose with a whirr. True to his sporting instincts, Jack pointed an invisible gun at the vanishing birds. Hurrah! thought he, there's something in this country after all. I had thought it was peopled only by ragged ruffians and scraggy goats and mangy camels. Partridges, I'll bet a dollar, he added, as a pair of birds rose from their very feet.

But the best thing in the bird line was yet to come. Signs of occupation became more numerous. Patches of cultivation dotted the landscape. Men were working in the fields, and little children peeped shyly but curiously from the doorways of squalid huts. Small flocks of sheep and goats depastured in the gullies and along the banks of the wady. The pious nomads halted at sunset, slid from their mounts to the earth, and, turning their faces to the east, postured themselves in prayer, repeating the formula addressed to the great Allah and His Prophet.

It was while the tribesmen droned their evening orisons that the air suddenly became vibrant with a flute-like yet joyous melody. As the sweet medley continued it increased in volume until it seemed to reach bursting-point, yet the exultant strains abated their sweetness in no wise: not a note of dissonance to jar the keenest sensitiveness. As the sweet concord struck the unaccustomed ears of the soldiers, gone in a flash from their consciousness was the pious whine of the tribesmen, and their souls were bathed in a flood of heavenly melody. Again and again it rose and fell in ordered cadence—the perfect poetry of sound, the faultless notes of sweetest music. Too entranced in the darkening eventide to speak, they became conscious that the ravishing sounds issued from a copse, and were made by a bird.

How long the sweet songster would have continued *his* orisons the enraptured listeners had no chance of determining, for, suddenly, one of the prone Bedouins rose from his praying attitude to his feet, seized a piece of jagged rock, and threw it with violence into the midst of the thicket, accompanying the act with a coarse malediction. In this way did the service of praise from the copse cease in order that the formal incantations of these pietists might proceed in uninterrupted flow.

"H'm," said Jock, "that's a pity. I suppose they were afraid it would upset their prayer-meeting—though I know which party I'd upset. I've never heard prettier singing than that which came from the throat of that dinky bird since I left Australia. Puts me in mind of a kookaburra."

"A kookaburra? A laughing jackass? Oh, my prophetic ears! Why, you unspeakable juggins, the old jackass is not to be named in the same breath with this chap, save for drawing a contrast in bird notes. Had you compared it with the bell-bird, the coachman, the scrub thrush-—but, a kookaburra! Do you know what bird it was which that rascal frightened into silence and flight? I'll bet a guinea it was a nightingale, the species they call a bulbul in the East. 'Kookaburra' say you? My christian aunt!"

"Sorry you take it that way, Major. No offence meant to that lovely little singer, who'd take the bun in any bird-singin' competition, if he chirped up to that form. What I meant was this. For instance, supposing a kookaburra was to start his laughing song out here, unexpected like, when you wasn't thinkin' of birds or anythin' else in particular, I wonder how you'd feel when you heard it!"

"Feel, Jockie, old man? I'd think his strident voice absolutely too heavenly for words. One toot from his windpipe would conjure up the old bush life in all its moods and movements. Oh, there's no doubt Jacky would be a real conjurer. I smell the gum leaves and the wattle fragrance at the very mention of his name. I seem to hear the echoing sound of the axe and the crash of falling trees. There goes a mob of brumbies careering up the valley with waving manes and tails atrail, snorting their defiance to the hunters! And there, too, goes a herd of grey and red kangaroos. Oh, for my old Winchester! And the homestead, and the stockyard, and the cattle! Can't you see that cunning old magpie perched on the gallows rail? Listen to the flutings of his rich, purple notes. Fit to match even with the bulbul's, aren't they, old—?"

"Stop! stop, Mr. Jack! For God's sake, stop!"

One glance at the distressed look on that hard-featured face was sufficient for instant silence. Unconsciously to himself, Jack's semi-humorous recital had become a bit of realism to his companion, late of Bobnawarra, and had brought on an attack of nostalgia.

CHAPTER III

HOW M'THIRST RECEIVED THE ATTENTIONS OF A BEDOUIN LADY

"WHERE in the mischief have we got to now?" exclaimed M'Thirst half an hour later as the party emerged from the darkness of the night, which had now set in, to the dim light of a settlement or small village. Lights faintly gleamed from open doorways as they shuffled over the cobbles of the narrow street, and the babble of voices saluted their ears.

"This, I suppose, is our destination," replied Jack. "At least I hope so. We've come far enough, to my way of thinking. Every mile in this direction, you know, takes us farther away from our fellows, which of course makes our return an increasingly difficult problem."

"You're right as usual, Major. If this old brute had any go left in him, I'd be for slewing him round and making a dash for it. No need to tell me it would be a mad act. It's a dead cert we'd not have a ghost's show of getting away."

"Wouldn't get fifty yards, old fellow, before we'd be headed. But for all that, we must keep our eyes well skinned for chances. They'll come, never fear."

As the Bedouins passed up the narrow, tortuous street they were kept busy replying to the sharp questions flung at them by the villagers. When, finally, they drew up at the other end of the village, before a cluster of low buildings, they were surrounded by a crowd of curiously excited people, who kept up a ceaseless jabber of inquiry.

Neither the sheikh nor his followers had been disposed to throw any light upon their doings as they passed along the street, but now the villagers were not to be denied. They stood in no awe of the marauders. The women in particular were pertinacious. After striving for a while to maintain a pose of dignified silence, it broke down before the ceaseless battery of questioning, which now began to be spiced with anger.

So persistent were the villagers, and so closely did they crowd the men, that the latter were unable to perform the duties of unsaddling. The rabble were determined their questions should be fully answered. The old sheikh had intended to describe their doings at a later stage, but now, making a virtue of necessity, after bawling out for silence, he set forth in picturesque speech the magnitude of their undertaking, the fearful perils they had encountered, their prolonged combat with the whole army of terrible Giaours, and the glorious victory achieved after decimating the ranks of the enemy. As an irrefutable proof of their prowess, behold their prisoners, the general and one of his high officers, sole survivors of the mighty host against whom they fought with splendid courage!

This recital, made in the darkness to itching ears, despite its wildly improbable nature, was accepted with loud demonstrations of approval. For well nigh an hour the old chief held forth on the brilliant exploit which he and his followers had so successfully carried out. It was the deed of their lives. Each of his followers was painted as a hero of the rarest kind. Each one had performed a feat —fully described—that would shed a radiance upon him and his children and his children's children for many generations.

In this florid style did the dramatist artfully weave an epic and act it out by speech and gesticulation, in a way that would have won admiration from a professional actor. Reserving his own part in this bloody fray to the last, with calculated art, he now sketched a picture in which he combined the strength of Samson with the valour and generalship of David. He swept his auditors off their feet, so to speak, by the power of his oratory. From the point of view of the stage it was a great success. Tumultuous applause greeted the actor when the series of ascents in his oratory reached the grand climax.

It did not seem at all strange to the listeners that the whole of their surpassing warriors should have returned; that not one of them bore a scratch; and that, beyond the two soldiers still astride the camel, these glorious fellows should have returned after such an encounter with no spoils of victory.

Before the effects of his fanciful and wholly fictitious description had begun to subside, the sheikh ordered the two prisoners to the ground. In obedience to this order the high and mighty Commander-in-Chief of the British forces, and his companion, slid to the ground in an undignified fashion, and were quickly surrounded by the motley mob. The awe of the Bedouins had not survived the recital. Until this, the British troops in general, and the Antipodeans in particular, were monsters of frightful mien, and had figured in many a weird tale. For the most part, they were giant Giaours who rode wild, untamed steeds, performed prodigies in battle, and habitually dined off human flesh. These were the fellows who had thrashed the picked troops of the Sultan; had driven them, pell-mell, across the desert from the Suez Canal to Rafa.

When, however, the villagers saw with their own eyes the two principal heads of the Giaour army, unadorned, pacific-looking, submissive to the slightest behest of the sheikh, of no abnormal size, their appearance was so different from the fire-eating, blood-drinking, gorilla-like specimens of fancy—the Bluebeards of their current tales—that their dread feelings quickly merged into an unconcealed contempt for them. They fearlessly pressed around them as they stood upon the ground, jostled them unceremoniously, pulled savagely at their clothes as if to tear them from their backs, spat in their faces, and, generally speaking, behaved in a fashion which was the reverse of friendly or polite.

The children, no less than the adults, gave expression to feelings of scorn and derision. The little ones, who only last night had been frightened into a nightmare through a recital of the bloody deeds of the men of the befeathered slouch hats, now, in imitation of their elders, called the captives by foul names. Picking up handfuls of dirt and pebbles, they shot their missiles at short range.

The two youths bore the abuse and mauling good-naturedly for some little while, but at length the limit of endurance was reached. They were in actual danger now from the pebbles and pieces of ragged rock that were being hurled with violence by practised hands. Already they had received some painful bruises. At last, M'Thirst, who had been shielding his face with his hands, as a protection from the pebble shrapnel, dived suddenly into a group of youngsters who formed the battery of assault, seized one of their number, holding him high in air, and, glaring the while in fearful grimace, made as though he would dash him to earth.

In a moment all the fears of the natives returned. A brood of wild-ducklings at the warning note of mother duck that danger is nigh, could not make themselves invisible with greater rapidity than did these Arab youngsters. So unexpected and quick Was Jock's movement, and so nearly did he approach their popular conception of a Giaour in appearance and act, that the crowd of men and women, including the sheikh's immediate followers, shrank back in dismay, uttering vehement appeals to Allah for protection. In less than ten seconds the jostling natives had changed from the offensive to the defensive. Not one of them had at that moment the courage to interfere.

How long this tableau would have held the people back it were hard to say. The picture of the long-limbed Australian, holding the wriggling, shrieking kiddie aloft, magnified itself sevenfold in the uncertain light of a couple of flickering lamps.

The moment of breathless suspense which followed the cries of fright—in anticipation of the act of throwing the child with violence to the earth—was changed into a great sigh of relief when the erstwhile champion of Bobnawarra brought down the child to the level of his head, bestowed a kiss upon his dirty face, and then placed him gently on the ground. No frightened rabbit ever scuttled more quickly to its warren than he to his mother's arms.

"Well played, Jock, old man! That was an inspiration. It did the trick all right. These good people were getting a bit too sultry. If I know anything about them, they will have learned their lesson."

"Well, we had to do something. It was, as you say, a bit sultry. I've got a lump as big as an emu's egg on my head," exclaimed Mac, with a rueful smile.

What Jack had said was true. The natives saw that they could take no liberties with these men, even though they were prisoners. The mother of the child which had been held aloft in a menacing attitude by Jock, had looked upon her precious one as lost. She instinctively closed her eyes to shut out the awful sight of her mangled darling. Her cars were attuned to receive the shock of the thud when his body struck the earth. But what did this prolonged sigh which rose all around her mean? Why had not the impending blow fallen? What meant these exclamations indicative of relief? Was it really possible—?

While not yet venturing to open her eyes, the distraught woman felt her knees firmly embraced by two small arms, while burrowed into her thighs was the face of a sobbing child. She knew now, in the fraction of a second, what had happened: her boy had been spared, and the next moment he was strained to her bosom. More than that. The revulsion of feeling rising in the mother's breast comprehends the prisoners. Under the influence of the gratitude which welled up in her heart she hastily set down her boy, and running up to the soldiers, who were still standing in the cleared area, she singled out Jock, and fell to the ground at his feet.

To say that Mac was astonished is to describe his sensations feebly. He was not altogether a stranger to the attentions of maidens. He had been classed as a desirable man by the Bobnawarra belles, who were not over-shy in giving or receiving pledges of affection. But this—! He gazed around in abject embarrassment while the woman grovelled at his feet, and held him round the legs in a firm embrace.

Quick to seize the humour of the situation, Jack broke out in hearty laughter, which became the less restrained as the look of helpless perplexity grew upon the face of his mate.

"For goodness sake, Mister Jack, call this creature off."

"Handle her gently, Jock," giggled his companion. "'Member she's only a frail wom—!"

"'Frail,' be jiggered! I'm fairly hobbled, man. Her arms are as strong as a green-hide lasso. 'Ere, missus, leave go of me, there's a good woman. I—I don't want any thanks. Never meant any harm to the kid. Oh, I say, turn off the tap of your water-tank, will you?"

"Jock, Jock, you'll be the death of me," spluttered Jack, as tears of laughter ran down his cheeks. "The lady thinks you're asking her to hold you tighter and to continue raining."

Judging from the contortions and loud whinings which came from the prostrate mother, it would seem as if that were the case.

"Well, then, Major, speak to her, will you? You can talk her lingo."

It was with difficulty that Jack could so far control himself as to speak to the woman. When at length he was able to master his mirth, he yielded to a suggestion from the demon of mischief, turning it to instant account. Stepping forward and bending over the woman, he shook her by the shoulders, speaking to her at the same time in short Arabic sentences. The effect was electrical.

Unloosing her grip of Mac's feet, she jumped to her own, and flinging her arms upward she closed them around the Westerner's neck.

This was too much for M'Thirst. Exercising the strength of his strong arms, he tore her hands from their clutch of his neck, and set her on the ground with more

" 'Ere, missus, leave go of me, there's a good woman."

firmness than tenderness. Before the woman could get over her surprise, Jack had taken her by the hand and led her to the women.

Dropping instantly to the trick which his mate had served him, M'Thirst's anger manifested itself in a sullen silence. It was a shabby trick. So thought Jack, and made instant amends. It was accepted after a short struggle of feeling, and soon the released victim of a woman's gratitude was able to laugh as heartily as his friend at the ludicrous figure which he cut under her close and unwelcome attentions.

CHAPTER IV

HOW THE BEDOUINS HELD THE AUSSIES

MANY weeks had now passed by since Jack Smith and Jock M'Thirst were brought to the little Bedouin settlement. During this time, though well treated from the Arabs' point of view, they were so well guarded as to find escape impossible, so far at any rate. This was not for want of planning, one might feel quite sure. The one thought of the prisoners was to get out of the hands of their captors and back to their regiment. They had devised many schemes that were not put into operation; not from lack of courage, but because the risks of recapture were too great. Jack's present policy was that of not appearing anxious to break gaol. A slackening in their gaolers' oversight was a necessary factor in the success of their scheming. He was determined that when they did make a bid for freedom, no chances of being retaken should be given. An unsuccessful attempt would only result in greater restrictions being imposed upon them, with increased vigilance on the part of their guards. All their plotting, therefore, was made under a mask of unconcern. Whether they were succeeding in throwing any particle of dust in the eyes of their captors they could only guess. They were inclined to think not, for, as the days passed by, they could not detect any relaxation of vigilance.

It must not be thought that they were constantly confined within stone walls. A certain amount of liberty was given them after the first few days of captivity. In the first place, instead of a stone dungeon, a mud hut formed their prison. They would not find escape there from a difficult problem. The walls which, so far, defied them, were the living walls of untiring watchfulness. In this the whole settlement took part. There was never a time during the day that they were unwatched. In this the children played a conspicuous part. They companioned their compulsory guests, never tiring of their company. Curiosity at the first prompted them; but even when curiosity staled, their watchfulness did not diminish.

At the beginning the youths encouraged these juvenile attentions. They had hoped thereby to transform foe into friend. Besides, the children made fun and beguiled the tedium of captivity. The children, on their part, lost all fear of the terrible Giaours. Their good-nature and readiness to join in their youthful sports made many admirers. If imitation be the sincerest form of flattery, as the wise people say, then both Jack and Jock had no reason to doubt their popularity. The children outvied the monkeys in mimicry. They quickly noticed any peculiarity in manner, action, or speech, and reproduced it in a droll fashion. Their impersonation, indeed, was the source of much pleasure to the prisoners, who neglected no opportunity of winning the confidence of the children. Yet, despite the real friendliness which existed between them, the young Arabs abated not one jot of their watchfulness. Not that it was paraded. Their instincts were as subtle as those of a feline. The little mouse will make break after break from the claws of puss under an impression of her inattention. Again and again will the poor palpitating victim be retrieved when it seemingly has passed beyond the zone of recapture. The wily cat's simulation of carelessness was shown to some extent in the bearing of these wild Arab lads.

Had the work of espionage been limited to the lads and lassies the problem of escape would not have been so difficult of solution. But there were, in addition, the women, who formed the second line, and behind them, the men, some of whom were always on hand. The sheikh, led by his predatory instincts, would be away for days at a time. A certain number of men, however, were always left, ostensibly to look after the stock and cultivation, which they attended to in a desultory fashion, but really to look after the prisoners.

It would appear to the uninitiated as if the steps taken to assure the detention of the captives were wholly inadequate, especially when the character of the imprisoned youths was token into account. If the Arabs were so determined to hold these distinguished soldiers of the British Army, why not place them in durance vile, and surround them with a guard, instead of adopting the loose method which gave them comparative freedom, with opportunities of escaping? Yet they could not have devised a more effectual way for barring their road to freedom. At night, it is true, they were locked up in a building which was barred from without, and to make assurance doubly sure, their feet were manacled with an iron chain and made fast to stocks. But in the daytime they had the freedom of the encampment.

More than once did the youths test the barriers, only to find that the smallest liberty taken against the surveillance brought the whole force of the villagers about them. That the demonstration was accompanied with laughter and expressions of village wit instead of anger and curses, served the more to prove to them that the elastic barriers were in reality more difficult to break than stone walls and armed guards. It certainly piqued the vanity of these resourceful bushmen that a parcel of Arab children and women should make their best laid schemes to go agley.

But a chain is only as strong as its weakest link. There would be found a defective link somewhere in this enveloping chain. It became visible to Jack one day while thinking out a new plan for circumventing the alert Arabs. The natives, whatever their character viewed from the moral standpoint of the Westerner, were scrupulous in their conformity to the daily practice of prayer. At sunrise and sunset Allah and Mahomet were remembered in this little out-of-the-way village, in the worship of posture and speech, by old and young. The daily imprisonment of the captives was regulated by these religious exercises. They were released from their cell after the morning's orisons and shut up again just before the evening exercises.

Here lay their one opportunity of escape. By some means or other must they be on the outside of their prison, and at a spot advantageous for the "jump off," at the hour of evening prayer.

What was to be done must be done quickly. At the present moment the sheikh and most of his men were away. Although the Arabs refused to give the captives an inkling of their fate, Jack gained something from the women. By eavesdropping he heard disjointed sentences, from which he was able to draw the conclusion that the Bedouins were approaching Turkish Headquarters with an offer to sell two highly-placed British officers whom they had captured. This they were doing cautiously and through intermediaries; for, if they applied in the first person, they knew that the Turks would demand the immediate production of their captives, regardless of any question of payment. They were only too well acquainted with the methods of their masters. No love had ever been lost between them, and if during the present war many of the scattered tribes were working in the interests of the enemy, it was not from any love, or even a sense of loyalty, but from fear and for pay.

Rapidly conning the situation and developing a plan, Jack sought his mate, who was just then drilling a squad of young Arabs, a pastime of which they never seemed to tire, and which afforded a considerable amount of amusement to M'Thirst.

"I say, Jock," exclaimed he in English, "dismiss these youngsters as soon as you can without arousing any suspicion, and join me at the ruin. I've got something to discuss with you."

So saying, he sauntered along the narrow, dirty street to the ruin of a stone building, which in all likelihood had been a granary in those far-off days when the Jews were masters of their own country, and carried out a system of close cultivation. Climbing over the debris at the foot of the broken wall, he perched himself on one of the highest portions, and awaited the coming of his mate with what patience he could command. For, having favoured the new idea as the most practicable of all those which had hitherto occurred to him, he felt that the more quickly it was put into operation the greater the chances of success would be.

While he sat waiting for Jock, several girls were playing about the ruin, while two or three women sat in an open doorway, gossiping. This surveillance was not discharged ostentatiously. To the uninstructed eye it would have appeared natural and undesigned. That it was part of the general plan was as well known to him as to the natives.

In the course of a few minutes Jock had marched his men up the street. Dismissing them outside the ruin, he speedily joined his companion on the wall. There was no attempt at secrecy. That would only awake suspicion. True, they might have delayed until night time, and discussed the scheme at an hour when all hostile ears were closed with the seal of slumber. But time was an object. The present was propitious. There was within Jack a growing feeling of confidence that Providence had made the opening, and that they would do well to seize it without loss of time.

With the noise and babel of playing children all around them the two youths discussed the plan of escape that had developed in Jack's mind. There was no lowering of tone or any attempt at secrecy in the conversation which ensued. The children were totally ignorant of the English language, and the prisoners had taken good care not to enlighten them. No one, unless he were within hearing, and knew English, would have judged from the quiet, natural tones, and the casual style of dialogue, that anything but the merest common places were being exchanged.

When M'Thirst joined Jack it was within an hour of sundown. The two talked over the plan for quite half an hour. Jack, who was sitting with his feet dangling over the wall, had his arms behind him, his hands resting upon the outer side of the crumbling wall. While he thus talked he threw the weight of his body upon his extended arms, as if to relieve his limbs for a moment from their contact with the hard, rough surface of the wall. This natural movement had disastrous results. One of the stones on which his hand rested was loose, and simply balanced by its weight. Disturbed by the pressure, it slipped out of its place, and Jack was thrown back across the wall, his head and shoulders hanging down on the other side. Before his mate could clutch him he had slipped over the wall, falling with violence to the ground, a distance of about twelve feet.

It so happened that the children, who were playing inside the ruin, did not witness the accident. Their attention was called to it by a loud exclamation from their drill-instructor as he precipitated himself from the wall into their midst, darted through an opening and round to the farther side where Jack lay motionless.

At the first moment the young Arabs thought that the prisoners were escaping. Raising a hue and cry, which brought the villagers up at a run, they rushed round to the front in pursuit, where they found M'Thirst bending over the body of his companion, calling him and vainly trying to shake him into some semblance of life. He had evidently fallen on his head, from the side of which blood was trickling. He was either stunned or killed. To the fearful imagination of the women and children he had been claimed by Azrael. "Alas! the poor Englees is dead." The Angel Of Pity looked out momentarily from their eyes. Jack possessed winning qualities, and had become an object of affection to these creatures, though they did not permit their tender feelings to weaken their watch. On the contrary, it made them more loath to part with him. But now the angel Azrael had taken the matter out of their hands! Well, poor Englees! But—what would sheikh Yacob say on his return? What would he do?

"One of the women brought a bowl of water."

But Jack was not dead. In answer to a call from M'Thirst one of the women brought a bowl of water. With this he laved the unconscious man's face and neck, as well as his hands. He had some trouble in forcing any water down Jack's mouth owing to his tightly clenched teeth. In a little while now he began to show signs of reviving. After a trembling of the eyelids he opened his eyes in a staring fashion, and muttered with his lips, "What's the matter?"

"He's as right as pumpkin," said Mac to the women, as soon as the unconscious man had made these movements. "He's a bit shook up, that's all."

"Here, matey," cried he, as he lifted the rapidly recovering major to his feet. "Stand up and see how you feel."

Jack responded to the invitation with what energy he could summon, but the moment he put pressure upon his left leg he let out a yell, and tumbled back in his companion's arms, who laid him on his back.

"It's my blessed ankle. I've sprained it badly. The pain's like red-hot wires."

Mac hastily yet gently removed Jack's left boot, and started bathing the ankle with cold water. After a little, Jack waved his hand to the onlookers, telling them not to be concerned, and that barring his foot he was as right as ninepence.

The women now turned homeward, and the children resumed their play, Jock, meanwhile, being constant in his attentions to the injured ankle.

It was while so engaged that the call to prayer resounded through the village. In a moment all work and play ceased, and the pious Mohammedans, big and little, turning their faces to the east, and kneeling forward, or lying prostrate as in the case of the children, performed their religious duty.

This accomplished, they rose to continue the common round, their first duty being to escort the prisoners to their cell. But where were the prisoners?

CHAPTER V

HOW JACK SMITH OUTWITTED HIS CAPTORS

NO one was more surprised than M'Thirst, when Jack, the moment the Bedouins were engaged in their devotions, sprang noiselessly to his feet and whispered to his comrade, "Quick! We'll get."

"But—Major—your ankle?"

"Ankle be shot! Come on!" pulling Jock to his feet. "Quick's the word and smart's the action. Now then, put every ounce into it."

"Well, I'll be everlastingly jiggered," breathed the sergeant, as he slipped round the angle of the wall on the heels of his leader. "He's got one on me this time and no mistake! Thought he'd crippled himself for a month!"

Jack had no time now to explain that his fall—with the accompanying insensibility and ankle sprain—was all part of his scheme of dissimulation in order to dull the sharp edge of the Bedouins' watch, as well as to delay their nightly duty of escorting them to the lock-up. Every particle of his breath would be needed for the sprint. As when the runner starts for the great race he loses sight of all else save the goal, so this runner had but the one thought—to make good his escape.

The moment the lads rounded the comer they were confronted with three possible routes of travel. The village lay in the form of a wedge between two deep wadies which converged at the north end within a hundred yards of the ruin, continuing northward from the junction on a larger scale. After running for some distance in this direction it took a sudden turn to the west.

Jack had made a study of the surrounding country. Not a feature had escaped his scrutiny. The wady on the left-hand side of the village ran from the junction in a south-westerly direction, while that on the right ran south a little distance, then formed an elbow and doubled back in its tortuous course towards the north-east. It was the last of these routes that Jack decided to take. Without pausing a moment to decide, he turned round sharply to the right, plunged down the bank of the wady, and tore along the bed, full pelt, with Jock hanging on his quarter.

They had just turned the elbow when loud cries sounded in their ears, by which they knew that the attempt to escape had been discovered. But they had won the first trick in the game. Their pursuers would be nonplussed. They must pause to determine the course of the fugitives. If, as was possible, they all kept together, it was two to one that they would choose the wrong track. Then again, if they split up into three sections it meant a weakening of their strength. Another point in the lads' favour was that the sun had well set, and could they keep going together for a short half-hour without being sighted, darkness would envelop them in its mantle. Still another thing stood to them—the character of their pursuers. At the outset the whole village would be hot-footed, but they must soon tail off. The children and the women lacked staying power. Before long it would be left to the young men and the well-grown boys.

The fleeing Anzacs surmised correctly. The Bedouins were nonplussed. Which way had the enemy fled? Many of the number, after a brief hesitation, followed the big wady which led due north. To their imagination it was the most likely route. Others turned to the left and followed the deep gully which led to the south. Only some four or five followed in the actual tracks of the fugitives. These, having turned the elbow unobserved, were following the winding gully which led in a north-easterly direction.

The twistings of the wady were all in favour of the youths. Had it maintained a straight course, they would have been sighted as soon as their pursuers turned the elbow. Nor did they intend that their late gaolers should ever sight them. But in this, as will be seen, they reckoned without their hunters, who were equally determined to sight and recapture them. The latter, also, had this advantage: they were better acquainted with the lay of the country. Jack's knowledge of it after all was confined to a narrow area, and before long he and his mate had passed beyond the bounds of the known.

Dusk was now rapidly approaching, and as they had been running at the top of their speed, they had good reason to believe that their chances of escape were momentarily increasing. They had now put a good mile between them and the village, and so far there was not the slightest sign of pursuit. Could it be that the Bedouins had all taken the other tracks, and so were quickly widening the distance between them? Or, if any had followed upon their tracks, might they not have given up owing to a failure to sight their quarry; or become daunted owing to the advance of the night?

The twisting wady now took upon itself the properties of a canyon. Its banks became sharp declivities which rose high on either side, at the same time narrowing in width. At this point it made almost a circuit owing to the intervention of a rocky hill, thus making a promontory of the land, with a narrow neck. It was while the fugitives were pounding along the rocky bottom on this circuitous detour that the trackers gained an advantage. Knowing every inch of the country and all the short cuts, they left the wady before it assumed its canyon-like form. Scrambling up the bank, they ran with what speed they were able across the neck of the promontory. So far they had followed upon a supposition, and there had been neither sight nor sound to confirm their belief. They would not be able to keep up the pursuit much longer. The pace had been hard, and dusk was settling into dark.

It so happened that both parties reached the point where the wady resumed its original course about the same time. The advantage of the lead, however, was still with the soldiers. As the hunters reached the bank they descried their quarry turning a corner about a hundred yards ahead. The sight so excited them that they gave a view- halloo—which was a blunder, for it gave notice to the pursued.

A feeling that the chase had been abandoned had been growing in the minds of the lads. While not yet easing the strong, steady stride into which they had fallen after the first burst, they had become easier in their minds. Every step onward was deepening the increasing sense of security. The cry of discovery which involuntarily broke from the human hounds cut short their self-congratulations. How many were grouped on the high bank they were unable to determine in the uncertain light. It was enough for them that several forms were scrambling down the steep bank, and in a few seconds would be upon them. They did not wait to count heads. Once more they put forth every ounce of strength.

It was now a case of endurance. Mettle alone would decide. No Marathon athlete ever showed more determination as he sped forward to the mark of his high prize than did these Australian bush boys. Nor were their pursuers far behind them in a firm resolve to capture. Had the lads known that the Bedouins numbered only four, of whom only one was armed, and that two of this number were juveniles, they would not have taken things so seriously. As it was, they were leaving nothing to chance. Should an encounter become necessary, well and good, but —the one form of strategy for the present was that of flight.

The hunters had been on the point of giving up, for their pursuit had been an uncertain one, and all this unwonted energy might be for naught. There was no guarantee that they were on the right track. The Bedouin is the last fellow in the world to exert himself unless there is a very good chance of an adequate reward. If upon reaching the wady alter their spurt across the neck of the promontory there had been no sign of the men they were seeking, they would have abandoned the pursuit. They had no stomach for a night adventure. Furthermore, they knew their prisoners to be strong, resourceful, and fearless. But the sight of the running men fired their ardour. They flung themselves into the wady, putting every ounce of energy into the pursuit. In all likelihood they would not have been so eager had the hunted been armed.

How long this hue-and-cry business would have lasted it were hard to say. The chances are that, had the soldiers rounded upon the pursuers, the latter would have turned tail instanter and scurried homewards like frightened rabbits to their warren. That tactic, however, had not occurred to them owing to their ignorance of the number following them. Had flight proved of no avail they would have fought their foes to the last ditch. The end of the flight was at hand, and came in a way unguessed by either party.

The darkness deepened to such an extent that the flight along the wady bed was accompanied with great risks, especially to those who were unfamiliar with the way. The ground at all times was uneven, and the bars of rock that intervened here and there were a menace to limb if not to life. So far the Australians had been very fortunate. Each had come an occasional cropper, but without any serious results, though their skin would show black in many places on the morrow. They could not afford to slacken their speed if they were to shake off the pursuit. They were fast approaching the limit, however, and would soon have to slow down. Of one thing they felt sure: they were drawing away from the Bedouins. Still, the distance between chasers and chased was not great, and any accident might delay them sufficiently for the others to overtake them.

As they thus sped on in the dark, the night suddenly became day. What on earth or in heaven had happened? No bolt from the clear blue ever was hurled with greater suddenness than the fireball which rushed through the air and fell at the feet of the soldiers. Both parties stood stock-still, with a dazed upward look. Then, before the flare died down, many forms could be seen lining the right bank of the wady. Another flare was thrown, brilliantly lighting the scene, and now a number of Turkish soldiers jumped into the wady, cutting off retreat and advance of pursued and pursuers alike.

Here was a case of out of the frying-pan into the fire with a vengeance. Better by far to have remained a while longer in the hands of the Bedouins than to be taken captive by the Turks. These were the first thoughts which flashed through Jack Smith's mind as soon as he grasped the situation.

"It's all up!" gasped M'Thirst to his companion as laconically as his breathless condition would permit. "We're nabbed sure enough this time. Blow these jolly Jackoes!"

"Bit of hard luck, old fellow, just as we'd about run our Bedouin friends to a standstill," replied Jack, with a whimsical smile, the while a couple of Turks laid no gentle hands upon them. "But buck up, old chap. 'A battle isn't wan till it's losht,' as Tim Hogan used to say."

CHAPTER VI

HOW THE LADS FELL INTO THE HANDS OF THE TURKS

THE Aussies had been so intent upon escaping from the hands of the Bedouins that they gave no thought for the moment to other possible dangers. Jack had canvassed almost every seeming avenue of escape. He had estimated the risks, chief of which was that of falling into the hands of the Turks. These gentry had overrun Palestine. They had garrisoned every place likely to be attacked, and had established lines of defence from side to side of the land. Their mobile units, too, were constantly on the move. But the risks had to be accepted.

When they bolted from the village all these risks were lost sight of in the concentration of mind and energy upon the job in hand—to elude their pursuers. But, after the first shock of surprise—occasioned by the unexpected way in which the Turks came into the game—had passed, it did not seem so strange to have fallen into the grip of the enemy.

The arresting Turks did not waste any time in the bed of the wady, but hustled their prisoners along the lines to the doorway of an officer's tent. The lads knew as soon as they saw the camp that they had been captured by a cavalry patrol. Jack quickly came to the conclusion that there were no Germans in the squadron, which was an immense relief. Uninfluenced by the German, the Turks' treatment of their prisoners had, on the whole, been humane.

Relieved on this score, Jack was greatly surprised at what he saw when ushered inside the door of the Turkish officer's tent. There, seated on a carpet at the feet of the captain, who was sitting on a stool, was the old sheikh Yacob. The officer, however, broke in on his stare of astonishment by addressing him in curt tones:

"Give an account of yourself!"

This imperative was given in perfect English. It caused the astonishment to take another turn. At first it was the sight of the sheikh in the tent. New it was through being addressed in his own tongue.

At the first glance the old sheikh did not recognise the soldiers as his late captives. They were standing in a half-light. But the moment Jack began to speak he recognised the familiar tones of his voice. Starting to his feet in great excitement, he laid hold of the two lads, shaking them with some violence, while he jabbered in Arabic.

"The old chap's got it in for us." said Jack, as the Bedouin fastened two hands upon his arms, swaying him to and fro. "I'll bet the villain's been negotiating for our sale to these fellows; but they've got us without parting with a piastre."

"Now then, friend Yacob, resume your seat on the carpet," continued he, as with a quick movement he grasped the sheikh's shoulders, and with a clever twist put him off the perpendicular, laying him full length upon the ground. "There, now, you wonderful hero, let the captain see the two distinguished British officers whom you captured off your own bat, after destroying their army at Rafa."

At this the Ishmaelite subsided and hung his head in confusion; for it was after magnifying his capture to the proportions in which he had visioned it to his own people on the night of his return to the village that the old sheikh had prevailed upon the Turkish officer to negotiate for the transfer of the prisoners. The Turkish Divisional Commander had made an offer a hundred times less than the demand, with the added proviso that the goods should prove equal to the description. He put a heavy discount on the fellow's statements, which, for the most part, he knew to be falsehoods. But at the same time it was possible that he had laid hands upon some officers of importance.

This accounts for the Turkish patrol and the presence of the sheikh in their company.

The captain showed his anger by telling the wrathful sheikh that if he didn't sit quiet and keep his mouth shut he would kick him out of the tent; and, furthermore, would order the men to thrash him off the lines; calling down at the same time upon his neck, head, body, and limbs all the prospective curses which he could conjure up at a moment's notice. The old man shrivelled up under this spray of invective, accompanied as it was with the threat of summary punishment. But his flashing eyes and wriggling form betokened no good to either Turk or Britisher, should opportunity serve.

This interlude ended, the Turk, mastering his anger, repeated his question to the youths. They had nothing to hide. Jack, who was spokesman, gave an unvarnished recital of their adventures, giving at the same time his own rank and that of his companion. There was nothing in the appearance of the Light Horsemen to indicate their rank. The Bedouins, true to their thieving instincts, had shorn their clothing of buttons and of every particle of decoration. The emu plumes, which were a distinguishing mark of the Queenslander, were now precious ornaments of adornment with the women, between whom daily fights occurred for their possession. Their dirt-stained and ragged clothes were far removed from the serviceable suits which they wore on ordinary occasions.

"So you're a major in the Australian Light Horse, and this chap's a sergeant?"

"That is so, captain."

"But you, a mere youth! Do you expect me to credit your statement?"

"It is true, nevertheless. I've been very lucky."

"But, man, I'm ten years older than you if I'm a day, and I only rank as a captain. Been all through that Gallipoli scrap, too!"

"It is clear you have not got your deserts," said Jack, with a smile. "With all your experiences and at your age you should at the least have been a brigadier."

"So I would but for those confounded Germans."

"But you don't mean to say that your allies were the means of—?"

"You see it was this way. By a bit of bad luck my battalion was incorporated in a German brigade. The beastly brigadier used to look upon us Turks as swine. He took a special dislike to me because I stood up to him when he blamed me for a silly piece of work done by one of his own officers. He marked me down and gave me a dog's life all through the campaign. But, praise Allah! we got rid of the dirty Huns, as you fellows call them, and rightly too, when we were transferred here. Take my word for it, there's no love lost between the Turks and the Germans. We know perfectly well that we're simply the tools of the Kaiser, employed to pull his chestnuts out of the fire. When we've done his dirty work we may rot for all he'll care."

If this disgruntled captain's deeds equalled his words, thought Jack, it's the commander of a division he should have been instead of a brigade. He could hardly smother his laughter: the whole thing was grotesque and bordered on the ludicrous. A few minutes ago he and Jock were racing along the wady for their very lives, with a pack of brigands at their heels, and, notwithstanding this, with a fair chance of escape. Then, as if by a, magician's wand, the scene was changed, and they were standing quietly inside a Turkish officer's tent, listening to an impeachment of the Kaiser and all things pertaining to Kaiserdom. Truly Aladdin's Lamp itself could not have wrought a more magical change.

So perfect was the captain's English that Jack began to question him about it, as soon as he had finished his grievances against the Germans.

The captain, nothing loath, informed him that he was born in England, and had received the best part of his education there, his father having been secretary to several of the Turkish ambassadors who had been accredited to the Royal Court. As a lad he had had a good time in England, especially in London; and even now he had no feelings against the land of his birth, though as a Turk there would be no failing in his loyalty to his race and creed.

"And now, Captain," said Jack, as soon as the Turk had finished his short autobiography, which he gave with relish, "the immediate and pressing question is, What are you going to do with us now that we have fallen into your hands?"

"That's easily enough answered. My instructions are to fetch you to Headquarters, provided, of course, that I'm satisfied you're worth the trouble; otherwise—" Here the captain made a significant gesture which was well interpreted by the prisoners.

"But you don't look as though you were awed by a sense of our importance," replied Jack, who was anxious to know more.

"I'm wasting no sentiment upon you," replied the Turk, with a sneer.

"Why bother the general with a couple of youngsters like us?"

"Would you prefer the alternative?"

"Not on your life!"

"Well, what do you want me to do, then?"

"Give us a sporting chance of working our way back to our own lines. Now that you have seen us and know how deliberately the sheikh has lied about us, and that the big prize pumpkin has shrunk to the dimensions of a small potato, you can surely have no further object in carting us along to your boss, who'll only rouse on you for your trouble."

"Yes?" interjected the Turk inquiringly.

"Let us loose, with the same advantage in point of distance that we held when you so dramatically appeared upon the scene."

"For consummate cheek you Australians take the bun."

"I'm afraid we'll never be hanged for an excess of modesty," returned Jack, with a smile.

"I've always heard that you were great sports," replied the captain, with a return to good humour, "and this proposition goes to show how deeply it is ingrained in your blood."

"It goes, then?"

"Goes to pot, you young innocents! But, I say, we'll have a lark with the old chap."

"A lark by all means," replied Jack, wishful to humour the Turk.

"Let us put your proposition to this dirty son of Ishmael. Do you speak Arabic?"

"Fairly well now. Have been struggling at it ever since I got to Egypt."

"Listen, Yacob," said the captain, turning to the Bedouin. "I find that you have been telling us a very big pack of exceedingly dirty lies. These youngsters are no prizes. They're simply tuppeny-ha'penny Billjims,"—Jack could not help flinching at this—"not worth the bother of carting to Headquarters. As a punishment for your mendacity and putting us to all this trouble for nothing, I'm going to tum them loose, giving them three minutes' start of your pack."

"What!" yelled the Bedouin in a tone of anger, as he struggled to his feet.

"I've done with 'em, d'you hear! You did not deliver them to me according to agreement. So, in turning them loose on the terms I have mentioned, I'm doing you a good turn after all. For, as sure as you are a filthy loafer and an unscrupulous liar, were you to accompany me to Headquarters your only reward would be a most terrific bastinado."

But the sheikh would have none of it. He stamped his feet, tore at his beard, while he poured forth from frothy lips a flood of Eastern Billingsgate. He had not lied. These men were high officers. He had virtually delivered the goods. Had not his own men literally chased them into their arms? No, no, no! By the great Allah and His holy Prophet, in whom both believed, he'd have his pound of flesh despite all the odds. He would hold the general to his bond.

Shylock himself never urged his plea with greater insistency than this Mohammedan, who saw his prizes about to slip from his greasy fingers.

"All right, Yacob," said the captain when he had drawn the Bedouin to the amusement of all three; for Jack had told Jock what the old fellow had said. "We'll settle this matter finally in the morning. In the meantime, you can clear. Out you go, sheikh!"

Placated by this deliverance, the sheikh, still growling, vanished from sight, and proceeded to where his men awaited him in fear and trembling; not without cause, for he poured out his vials of wrath upon them as only an Eastern is capable of doing.

The Turkish captain had not the slightest thought of giving back the prisoners to the Bedouins, or of granting them the "sporting chance" which Jack asked for. Nor, for that matter, did Jack expect to be taken seriously when he made the request. It was simply a try-on. He felt, however, that as long as they remained in the custody of the patrol they would be well treated. Perhaps, after all, the chances of escape would be increased instead of diminished.

The change of gaolers made no alteration to the purpose of the lads. The one settled determination of their wills was to win free from their captors, whoever they might be. They had been hopeful when they skipped from the Bedouins. Those hopes were more than justified, for they now saw clearly that nothing could have prevented their escape from the clutches of these fellows, but for the intervention of the Turks. Ah, well, it were worse than useless to cry over spilt milk! Severe as the jolt had been to their high hopes, they were not indulging in any pessimism.

As soon as the captain had dismissed the sheikh he turned to the two youths. He performed an immediate *volte-face*. The suave, good-humoured tones of a moment ago were replaced by a curt, official style.

"Consider yourselves prisoners. Any attempt on your part to escape will be visited by the severest penalties. If, however, you will give your parole, it will be accepted."

"Thank you, Captain; I prefer to be treated as an ordinary prisoner. I could claim separate treatment, as you know, on account of my rank. That I surrender, as I have no wish to be separated from my sergeant."

Answering by a short nod, the Turk gave instructions to the guard, who, throughout the interview, had stood behind their prisoners.

As they were in the act of leaving under escort, Jack spoke a final word to the captain.

"Would you kindly order us something to eat? We've had nothing to eat or drink for fully a year."

"I see that you are true to your type," said the captain, his severe look breaking into a smile. "The one thought of you Billjims seems to be—tucker."

No more was said at that moment. The captives were speedily taken to a guard-tent. Later on in the evening their supper arrived. The hungry Australians made no complaint either of the quality or the quantity of their food.

CHAPTER VII

HOW THEY REACHED TURKISH HEADQUARTERS

IT was late in the succeeding day when Jack Smith and Jock M'Thirst, in the custody of the Turkish patrol, reached enemy Headquarters. Their way led through the hill country of Judea. The young Anzacs had no cause for complaint in regard to their treatment during the day's travel. They had the free use of their limbs, and each was mounted on a decent steed. They rode in the centre of the squadron, But beyond that no restriction was placed upon their freedom. The Turks ran no risk in this, for escape under present conditions was impossible. Strangers in a strange country, unarmed, surrounded by well-armed and well-mounted cavalry, to make the attempt would amount to inexcusable folly.

No one knew this better than Jack. No one could be quicker than he to weigh the chances of winning clear by any ruse they might adopt. He saw, too, with some sinking, that every hour's travel was sensibly increasing the difficulties of escape. Any rash attempt would be surely followed by the curtailment of the privileges they were now enjoying. The captain, who last night showed himself to be friendly and considerate, might easily be worked up to the severest measures. With all his English birth and upbringing, he remained an Eastern. Let his anger burn against them, and this Turk who yesterday talked like an English schoolboy would set no bounds to his brutality.

No, there was not a ghost's show of escape! No good acting the role of the caged wild bird which, in its vain attempts to escape, breaks its wings against the

"

impregnable bars. M'Thirst, on the other hand, with a confidence born of his rude strength and an unvarying contempt for the Turk, would long ago have made an attempt, but to every suggestion Jack gave a prompt negative.

But while Jack dismissed the idea of escape as an impossibility when on the march, his alert brain, none the less, was busily engaged. He scanned the country through which they were passing. Not a landmark escaped the scrutiny of his wonderful eyes. His ductile brain registered a mental map of the route, which would unroll itself at the dictate of his will. He looked for no miracle, believing strongly that God helps those who help themselves.

The country became more and more fertile as they progressed. Wheatfields were passed in close succession. Black and brown Bedouin tents dotted the landscape. Flocks of sheep and goats, straggling camels and donkeys, and small herds of cattle browsed on the hillsides and in the intervening valleys. Women and children moved about the tents, while donkeys were passed at intervals in charge of women, laden with brushwood for fuel.

The thing which impressed Jack most, as his eye took in the general appearance of the country, was neglect. As against this everything pointed to a rich past; to a period when Palestine justified its ancient name—"A land flowing with milk and honey." The dilapidated remains of walls, building, reservoirs, bore witness to the Golden Age of Palestine, when, in other hands, close cultivation produced rich harvests, and towns and villages throve upon the fruits of agriculture, and the flocks and herds covered the thousand hills of the Holy Land. As his busy brain constructed periods in the far-away past, deduced from the remains of broken walls, ruined temples, fragments of pottery, and the miscellaneous debris of bygone centuries, which bore witness to a high civilisation, a pure religion, wealth, and intellectual greatness—when the Hebrew system was at its zenith, and sent forth its proud challenge to the still more ancient civilisations—the actual condition of the land under Turkish misrule and Bedouin neglect made a painful impression upon him.

About midday the column passed through a Zionist settlement, which, despite the exactions of the Turks, gave ample evidence of what the land was capable of under systematic cultivation. Barley, wheat, and rye brought forth abundantly. Well-cared-for orchards and vineyards were laden with many fruits. Vegetable gardens were fat and flourishing. It was characteristic of the Turks to despoil the gardens and orchards as they rode along the way, offering neither payment nor civility. Yes, undoubtedly, salvation will have come to Zion when the dead hand of the Ottoman rule has been once and for ever removed from the oppressed peoples of that ancient land.

Although the patrol made many deviations, for they had other duties beside that of taking the Britishers to their Headquarters, Jack knew from his knowledge of the ordnance maps of Palestine that they were advancing to the heart of the Judean hills. He sought detailed information from the soldiers surrounding him; but, although his questions were artfully put, they were fruitless. The Turks, according to their mood, either made no acknowledgment of having heard his questions, or answered in terms of contemptuous epithet, or gave evasive replies. Before long it became evident to him that they were acting under instructions, and were not to he drawn.

During the course of their travel they were in frequent touch with other patrols, and on two occasions passed within sight of two large camps of infantry. Although denied any knowledge through the medium of his ears, Jack was using his eyes to good purpose.

The youths were deeply impressed with what they saw. Every mile, from the point of view of a fugitive bristled with difficulties and dangers. Should they succeed in breaking from their confinement, they would have to run the gauntlet at every step of the way. In view of the subsequent results it had become evident to them that they followed the wrong road when they broke from the Bedouin settlement. Had they fled along the south-west track instead of the north-east, they would not have run into these enemy entanglements. The dangers of that way were surely small compared with those which had now become an encompassing net. Well, they must make the best of a bad bargain, and keep on smiling. Perhaps after all they'd made no mistake, and things would turn out dinkum. At any rate, pessimism never yet built a bridge, nor opened a door of escape. That spirit led to defeat and death. So, while not indifferent to the increasing difficulties of escape, the lads were ready at the first opportunity to accept all the risks and hazards.

The sun was well on his westering wheel ere they reached their immediate destination.

The first intimation of this was conveyed in the shrill shriek of a railway whistle which came to them as they ascended a steep hillside.

"Listen to that, Major!" exclaimed M'Thirst at the sound.

"Sounds like civilisation, doesn't it? Guess we're about at the end of our jaunt. Unless, that is, they rail us to Jerusalem. Wouldn't it be a prime lark, eh?"

"I'm not pining for a sight of Jerusalem. It's all right, of course, but I'd a jolly sight sooner see the lines of our regiment, an' hear the chiacking of our fellows."

Jack was on the point of replying to this natural but doleful statement, but forebore. He had other thoughts in his mind than that of sight-seeing, much as he would love to enter the gates of the Holy City. A policy had shaped itself in his mind to this effect—Get all the possible information of the disposition and strength of the enemy's forces, while in their hands. The farther they travelled towards the Turkish centre the more readily would they be able to estimate his power. Should it be their fortune to be taken to Jerusalem, well, the chief interest at the present time would not lie in the sites and relics associated with Bible history. It would go hard if he did not turn the occasion to the good of his own side.

He needed no telling that he would go to Jerusalem as a prisoner, and in that relation his chances of gaining information would be of the scantiest nature. He knew what would come to pass in a general way. But he had no intention of allowing these untoward circumstances to thwart him. In short, he was an incurable optimist. There was never a place of confinement from which there was no way of escape. Stone walls, iron bars, barbed wire, prison guards, will all yield to a determined will.

Anyone who knew Jack Smith knew perfectly well that conceit and he were poles asunder. Yet for all that he believed in himself, and in his star. He never lost faith. His was the faith which moves mountains; which achieves the impossible; the faith which has been in the world from the beginning, and by which all great things have been wrought in the course of human history. It was his good fortune to be in the line of succession to those mighty heroes of faith who subdued kingdoms, administered justice, shut the mouths of lions, and won strength from weakness.

When the squadron reached the summit of the hill they paused a moment before descending the long slope which led to the plain beneath. The Australians gazed with delight upon the prospect, which varied in appearance and colour from the rugged hills in the distant scene, which were bathed in brilliant light—the dying effort of the setting sun—to the broken plain and the intersecting gullies, which glowed in the mellow light of eventide.

A military camp lay at a distance of about a mile, abutting the railhead. Ponderous buildings and a system of trenches, with the inevitable wire entanglements, covered the flat, which was flanked on either side by deep gullies. All this was easily discerned and keenly scrutinised by the two youths during the short halt on the summit. The thought of escape was never out of their minds, and every surface feature of the camp was scanned and remembered.

All through the day the leader of the squadron had kept aloof from the prisoners. He remained at the head of his column throughout the journey, and Jack wondered why he maintained this aloofness. It was in striking contrast to his behaviour of the previous night. Then he appeared glad to have a Britisher to talk to. He was free in his confessions of his regard for Englishmen, and the good times he had had in London when a boy. Nor was he slow to express his dislike for the Germans. Why, then, this change of face? Had it occurred to him that he had been too free, and had opened his mouth too wide when cursing the Turkish alliance with the Huns? Whatever the cause, Jack was strongly inclined to think that his reference to Teutonic influence, made on the impulse of excited feeling, was answerable for the avoidance.

Jack had reckoned on further conversation, for a Turk who had declaimed so unreservedly might prove a gold mine of information under skilful treatment. When, therefore, an order came from the captain that they were to join him immediately, the two youths became bright with anticipation. A mark of favour on entry to Headquarters would go far to help them.

Great was their disgust when, on appearing before the captain, he not only omitted to extend to Jack the salute that was due to an officer of his standing, but gave him a contemptuous stare, which was followed by a curt command to ride immediately at his rear. Putting his horse in motion, he led the way down the slope at a trot.

"What does he mean by this, I wonder?" said M'Thirst.

"Don't know, Mac, unless it's a bit of embroidery. Don't forget we're two highly-placed British officers; almost the sole survivors of our army."

"Is he going to hand on that dope to his chief?"

"You can never tell, Jock, what's in the mind of an Eastern. Judged superficially, I should say that he has arranged a triumphal entry, and that an imaginary band is banging into his ears, *See the Conquering Hero Comes!*"

CHAPTER VIII

HOW THEY LIVED LUXURIOUSLY, AND HOW M'THIRST RECEIVED A SHOCK

CONTRARY to their expectation, the prisoners were not immediately brought before the general. Instead, they were taken to a stone building which stood at some distance from the central group that formed the Headquarters of the Divisional Staff.

They were surprised at the quietness of their entry to the camp. Not only was there an entire absence of anything approaching the theatrical: no one took the slightest interest in their arrival. They had thought from the disposition made by the captain as he descended from the hill to the plain, that something of a dramatic nature was being prepared.

But, within a few yards of the outermost barrier, the troops were halted. A few short words of command followed, and the entire squadron broke from the head of the column, leaving about twenty men with the captain. Wheeling sharply to the right, the former followed a well-defined road which led due north, while the captain, with the barest acknowledgment of the guard, passed into the compound with the remnant of his troops. Swinging to the left as he approached the central buildings, he halted before the isolated structure.

Hitherto his demeanour had been that of aloofness, not to say sullenness. He had held no communication with the prisoners during the long march. But as he halted his men his mood changed with the swiftness of lightning.

"You are glad, I am sure, to have come to your journey's end," said he, addressing the lads in excellent English, and with a pleasant smile. "I think you'll find things pretty decent inside."

The change from a sullen silence to an amiable mood and gay speech came as a shock to those addressed. From the demeanour of the captain they had augured severity, if not ill-treatment, when they should have come to the end of the march. And now they were inclined to treat his friendly remarks as a piece of sarcasm.

As they followed him into the hut their surprise increased. It contained only two rooms, but they were of fairly large dimensions. The front room was evidently used for general purposes. There was a good-sized table in the middle, while a large settee occupied a space on one side, and on the other were a few comfortable chairs. In the room behind, which served as a bedroom, were two soft couches which did duty as beds. In one corner was a washstand, and in the other a bath, and—what the lads had been strangers to for ages, so it seemed—some clean towels.

"I say, Captain," exclaimed Jack, after a brief survey of their surroundings, "this looks pretty comfortable. To be frank, it isn't exactly what we were looking forward to. Is this a tribute to the high rank of Jock and myself?"

"My advice to you, my young friend, is to take the good that the gods provide without question."

"Taken without any further demur," replied Jack, with a laugh. "Compared with our lodgings in the Bedouin camp this is heavenly."

"Your supper will be over in a brace of shakes," continued the captain. "I'll see you some time tomorrow. Good-night, and a dreamless sleep."

With this good wish the captain disappeared through the doorway. The next moment he was clattering away with his guard, and the lads were seemingly left alone.

"Well, if this doesn't beat any fairy tale ever told, Jock! The quarters aren't palatial, it is true. There's nothing Oriental about 'em either. But it's dinkum for all that. Why, here's a fireplace with wood and coal all fixed ready for kindling. And, look here! Blest if on this sideboard there aren't stacks of cigars, cigarettes, pipes, tobacco, liquors, and what not. Shades of Aladdin! Say, Jock, haven't you got a word to say?"

"Say? Blowed if I know, Mister Jack, what to say. 'Pears to me that there's something more in this than meets the eye. Looks to me like a bloomin' trap, as the dingo said when he come on a dead, fat lamb lying across his track."

"Why, what's this?" continued he, as a couple of servants came through the doorway, bearing a tray laden with eatables that would have charmed an epicure. To the eyes of the hunger-bitten youths it seemed a feast fit for the gods.

Lighting a large lamp that stood in the centre of the table, the servants proceeded to lay the table. "I tell you what, Jock. First thing for me is a bath. I'll hurry so that you can have one before supper." In less than a minute Jack was splashing the water with the noise of a paddle steamer.

By the time the two had performed their ablutions supper was ready. They had just got going when Jock, whose mind had been pursuing a train of thought, stopped short, exclaiming:

"S'pose the food's poisoned?"

"What in the name of strychnine makes you think that?"

"Well—er—er, blest if I know!"

"Look here, old chap! Do you think for a moment that these fellows would go to all the trouble of taking us prisoners, and yanking us to their Headquarters, simply to murder us, when they could have done it quite as effectually where they found us? Or given Yacob the job, which the old rascal would have been delighted to do for a consideration? Poison us? Not on your life! The idea is too preposterous to be entertained for a moment."

"Begum, so 'tis, now I come to think of it."

"Well, then, let's wade in. We'll halve this roast fowl to start with."

"I say, Mister Jack, isn't this dinkum coffee?"

"Delicious, old man. *Café au lait*, as the Frenchies call

it. Made with milk. I say! suppose after all you're right, and these treacherous beggars have poisonous designs in this swell feed! It's the coffee they generally dope, you know. Come to think of it, there's a peculiar flavour about this stuff. Doesn't it taste bitter to you?"

Jock, who was just putting the second cupful of the fragrant *Mocha* to his lips, arrested the upward tilt of the cup, and stared at the grave face of his companion. But try as he would to maintain his gravity, Jack's twinkling eyes betrayed him.

"Bitter, say you? Yes, indeed. I noticed it in the last cup. It's as bitter as—coffee!" So saying, M'Thirst drank off the contents of the second cup in two swallows, and handed it along for a third filling.

Generous as the spread had been, when the eaters had satisfied their hunger, the fragments remaining would have hardly served a bandicoot for a snack.

"Wonder if they're going to lock us up for the night?"

"The very thought that was crossing my mind. Not likely to let us roam at large, eh?"

"Wish I could think 'em fool enough for it. I bet they've guards stationed all round."

"If they have they've been jolly quiet. Haven't heard the sound of a footstep since the waiters went. Hold on a bit. I'll have a squint round."

Rising as he spoke, Jack moved to the open doorway, expecting to see at least one guard. To his surprise no one was in sight. Passing out, he sauntered round the house without meeting a solitary sentinel.

"If this doesn't beat the band!" said he on re-entering the house, after completing the circuit.

"There's not a soul in sight, except those moving about Headquarters."

"Well, then, what's to hinder us flitting?"

"A thousand things, you old juggins. That we're not guarded in the ordinary way is a proof that they've taken precautions which make that usual practice unnecessary. You may be as sure as you are of anything in this world that these fellows haven't brought us here for the fun of the thing. There's a method in their madness. But what their object is I cannot say. At the present moment it is more than I can attempt to guess."

"Perhaps you're making a mystery out of nothing."

"Quite possible, but highly improbable. What do you make of it all?"

"Strikes me it's only carelessness. The Turks aren't Germans, are they? If this was a Boche camp, it's a million to one that we'd be locked up, with double guards at every corner of the house, to say nothing of a platoon or two inside. But Jacko is a careless cuss all right, as I've heard you say a score of times. Never does to-day what he can put off till to-morrow."

"Yes. That's true," said Jack meditatively.

"He's like the niggers for that. Tell you what. If you think they've forgotten to put on guards, test it. The proof of the pudding, you know."

"Meaning—?"

"Exactly."

"Righto."

Moving without another word to the doorway, M'Thirst stood for a minute or two in a lazy attitude, mostly gazing into the star-studded sky, while he lit a cigarette taken from a packet which lay on the table. That done, he moved outward at a slow gait, hands in pockets, having assumed a pose the least suggestive of any thought of skipping. In this way he meandered in a seemingly purposeless fashion, all the time working away, not only from the hut, but also from the main buildings, which were partially lit up. In this way he gradually neared that portion of the camp which bordered on the entrenched wady. Not a soul did he meet in these wanderings, nor for that matter did he hear the sound of any movement save a shuffling noise in the trenches, together with the faint murmur of voices. M'Thirst was not a little pleased with himself. He seldom cared to oppose any of Jack's opinions. But in this case he was making good his own statement as to Turkish negligence.

Then, suddenly and startlingly, when he had crept to

within a few paces of the bank, a squad of men rose from the earth, while the whole arena was lit up with a flash of brilliant light.

Jock stood in his tracks as if petrified, with eyes a-stare as if at an apparition. Then, as suddenly as it came, the light vanished, the contrast being gross darkness. During this tableau not a sound was made on either side.

Jock's simple mind, while prosaic enough in many directions, was not proof against this bizarre happening. He stood speechless, almost breathless, his limbs taking on the nature of goose-flesh. In addition, a fearsome feeling suffused his being. This sort of thing was new to him. Every second in the dark seemed an hour. At last, after a few moments—though it seemed an eternity to him—he was overmastered by his fear and bolted incontinently back to the hut.

When he burst through the doorway the first thing he saw was Jack laid out on the settee, his body going through a series of contortions. In a flash all M'Thirst's troubles had vanished. He stood gazing at his companion with a feeling akin to terror. Had his best friend gone mad?

Or was he poisoned? Was this convulsion, this body-twisting, these awful grimaces? Were they poison spasms? Surely they were the victims of a devilish plot!...

But Jack was not poison-infected. He was in a fit, it is true, but it was a fit of hilarity. He had been a watcher of Jock's manoeuvres, as far as his keen eyes enabled him to follow him in the darkness. And when he had vanished from sight, he waited with a good deal of curiosity for developments. That he would continue to wander at his sweet will, unhindered, he did not for a moment dream. When, finally, the bright flash lit up the scene, revealing the squad of Turks face to face with the Bobnawarra champion—whose amazement was made plainly visible in the dazzling light—the ludicrous side of it made an irresistible appeal to his humour. A few moments later, Jock found him the victim of uncontrollable mirth.

Hot anger surged through M'Thirst and mantled his face. Unable to appreciate the humour of the situation himself, he was on the point of giving vent to his feelings in strong language. He did not let go, however, and this evident restraint sobered Jack more quickly than any string of red-hot expletives could have done.

"It's all right, old man," cried he, wiping the tears from his eyes. "Don't take any notice of me. It's a century since I last saw a display of *tableaux vivants*, and when you and the Jackoes faced one another in the brilliant light I could see at once that they were even more surprised than you. It's them I've been mostly laughing at. Oh, crumbs! If you'd only seen it as I saw it!"

"Glad the fright wasn't all on my side, anyway," replied Jock, mollified by the major's way of putting it. "I tell you my heart sank into my boots when the light flashed half a dozen Johnnies' ugly mugs in my very face. Begum, a feather'd have knocked me over. I say, aren't the varmints cunning?"

"Perhaps, after all, it was purely accidental. The man at the flashlight might only have been practising; or did it simply as a precautionary measure."

"But how do you account for the men springing up under my very nose?"

"Well, after all, there's nothing so strange in that. It was probably a patrol, or men who had been relieved. The chances are that the light would have flashed just the same, and the men would have been at that particular spot, even if no such being as Jock M'Thirst existed. If you'd only thought to give the Bobnawarra yell, the beggars would have hit the trail with a promptitude and a zeal that nothing but the Mediterranean could have stopped."

"Maybe. But if they was half as scared as I was, they'd have done the same as this chicken, without a whisper."

"Anyhow, Jock, you didn't scout for nothing. You drew the enemy. What say starting this fire? It's getting quite nippy. I'm going to try one of the general's cigars."

In a few minutes both lads were sitting over a bright fire, and puffing smoke in great contentment. The contrast between their condition now, and that of the same hour the previous evening, was so great as to create doubts as to its reality. Then they had just been "grassed," so to speak, by the Turks, at the very moment of escape from the Bedouins. Now they were receiving the treatment of honoured guests. How long this delectable experience was going to last was a question not to be pressed unduly. They were too comfortable to speculate on the matter. Why take any thought for the morrow? Sufficient unto that day would be its discomforts and perils.

For the present—the well-cushioned seats, the bright fire, the fragrant incense! And, by and by, the soft couch and pleasant dreams!...

CHAPTER IX

HOW THE GENERAL'S TREATMENT OF HIS CAPTIVES BECAME AN ENIGMA

JACK SMITH awoke in the first flush of the dawn from a deep, dreamless slumber. It is at this time that the mind is in its most receptive mood. The happenings of yesterday imaged themselves with clear-cut distinctness in his brain. Nebulous thoughts assumed concrete form. The change in the Turkish captain's deportment; the unusual provision for their comfort; the measure of liberty accorded them —did not, he was now sure, spring from the fancy portraits presented to the old general by Sheikh Yacob. The superior accommodation was not a tribute to rank. Neither could it be attributed to the humanity of the Turks. The idea of this treatment of their prisoners —extending beyond ordinary comfort until it reached the point of luxury—being viewed as an element of Turkish humanity, was more than ridiculous. It was a prime joke.

But the Turks were not given to joking in the treatment of their prisoners, unless it happened to take the form of torture. The splendid treatment so far meted out to them as prisoners of war was but a piece of *camouflage*—a sprat to catch a mackerel. Behind all this seeming deference and generosity was a purpose, and this purpose became clear to Smith in the dawn of the early morning. The Turks were going to use them.

As to the specific object they had in view, that was not so clear. There were two things, however, either of which would reasonably account for their special treatment. The Turks were seeking information, and it was quite reasonable to suppose they would try to coax it out of their prisoners. Facts of importance were to be obtained from them, and the high quality of the food, the fine cigars, the choice wines—all this was the lubricant to make the pumps work easily.

Then, again, it was at least possible that the enemy was bent on winning them from their allegiance under alluring promises. This at the first flush appeared wildly improbable, and was rejected, only to return, until it found a lodging-place. Jack remembered that bribery was a universal weapon among all Easterns, and that it was regarded as a fine art by the Turks. To their way of thinking every person was buyable. Self-interest was the leading individual motive, and it was therefore only a question of price to secure the adhesion of a person to a side.

"All right, Mr. Jacko," muttered Smith. "It'll be interesting to watch your movements. But what if the pump won't work after all the oiling? And what, I wonder, is to be the measure of your reward for a change of uniform?"

"I say, M'Thirst," shouted he a few minutes later to his sleeping companion, whose intermittent snorts had become a source of irritation, "ring off those beastly snores!"

"A—a—a—wassamatta?"

"What's the matter, you old juggins?" cried Jack, as he heaved a pillow at the head of his mate.

"Stop that racket. We've got a couple of visitors. Jump up and let 'em in."

"All right!" drawled Jock sleepily, as he dragged himself out of bed, while he rubbed his sleep-drugged eyes. Then, staggering forward to the back door, which faced the east, he unbolted it.

Throwing the door wide open, he gazed around stupidly. There were no visitors that he could see, and the only figures in sight were some Turkish soldiers in the distance cooking their breakfast.

"Thanks, old chap," said Jack. "That's fine!"

"What's fine?" asked Jock, looking round.

"And what do you mean by visitors?"

"Oh, they've come in. Don't be alarmed, they aren't ghosts. Fresh air and sunshine, my boy, been waiting outside for hours while you've been snoring."

The two proceeded to dress; and after a few minutes Jack said:

"There's just two things the beggars have forgotten to provide us with."

"Yes?"

"Razors and toothbrushes."

"Begum, you're right! At any rate the razors. I've acres of scrub on my cheeks that I'd like to clear."

"You do look like a sundowner on the wallaby," remarked Jack, as he surveyed his comrade's face and marked the heavy growth of beard which hung pendent from his cheeks. "I'll ask the captain for the loan of his razor as soon as he comes."

When the captain paid his promised visit, however, the razor was forgotten. It was remembered later as Jack stood before the general.

While waiting for breakfast the lads surveyed the area, taking in every bit of their surroundings, as far as they were observable to the eye. They noticed clearly now what they had failed to observe in the gathering dusk of the previous night upon their arrival at the camp. Sentries were posted at short intervals inside the inner line of defences. This accounted for the sudden appearance of the men before the astonished Jock last night. But it still left the conjunction of the men and the flashlight an unsolved puzzle. Whether accident or design, was still a matter for speculation.

Although it would appear that the lads had the freedom of the camp, they did not trade on it. They kept within a few paces of the hut, putting on a casual air so as not to provoke any suspicion. None the less were they keenly bent upon constructing a practical plan of escape which might be put into operation at a moment's notice.

Shortly after breakfast the captain, true to his promise,

paid a visit to them. He was in his most amiable mood. He told them that he was quartered at the main camp, about four miles distant. Jack, by casual questions, elicited the composition and numbers of the Turks, which, if true, made a truly formidable array. This, the captain said, was one of many such camps in well-selected positions. The captain chatted unrestrainedly upon military matters. As a matter of fact he overdid it. Jack quickly detected in his volubility and confidences the arts of a dissembler. His free speech was of a piece with the exceptional treatment meted out to them. He professed a great admiration for the British, and a love for England. His remarks about Turkish defences and numbers, together with his hail-fellow-well-met manner, while evidently done with a design, did not deceive Jack. Yet he readily fell in with the mood of the captain. He talked freely about the desert campaign. But, while giving many particulars with regard to British movements and the composition of their forces, he carefully avoided anything that could not have been learned with the smallest amount of trouble, and in all probability was well known to the Headquarters Staff, both Turk and German.

Jack's *camouflage* was cleverer than the captain's, so artfully did he skirt the things that really counted, while magnifying and elaborating the things which almost any busybody might find out and be little the wiser for knowing.

At length, after glancing at his watch, the captain referred to the direct object of his visit.

"Oh, by the by, the general requests your presence at Headquarters at ten o'clock, and I promised to bring you across."

"Very kind of the general, I'm sure, and very nicely put," said Jack, with a smile, companioned with a wink designed to be seen only by M'Thirst.

"I'm sure both the sergeant and myself will have the greatest pleasure in meeting your illustrious chief."

"The command doesn't extend to the sergeant," replied

the Turk, with a meaning glance towards Jock, as if to say, "This fellow doesn't count a doit with the general."

"I see," said Jack, after a moment's pause. "Mac, you'll have to forego the pleasure of facing the general, who'll thus miss the chance of meeting my brilliant chief of staff."

"You Australians are incorrigible jokers," remarked the Turk, with a shrug, as he rose. "I'll return in half an hour, when you'll be ready to accompany me."

A hard, menacing tone had crept into the captain's voice as he made this announcement.

Within the time mentioned he returned to the hut, and Jack, who had nothing to prepare, was waiting in readiness for the ordeal of facing the divisional chief.

Passing through the general entrance, at which a guard was posted, the two men proceeded along a passage which presently led into a large room. Here were several tables, some of which were being used by Staff officers, who were poring over maps, or engaged in writing. As they passed through this room some of the officers looked up, and one or two of them called the captain by name. Jack scanned the room as he followed the Turk. The majority of officers, he saw at a glance, were Turks; but a group of three in a corner, engaged in a warm conversation, were undoubtedly German. Apart from the uniform they wore, their speech betrayed them.

Knocking at a side door, before which an orderly was stationed, the captain stood until a voice within bade him enter. Then, opening the door, he entered the room, with Jack at his heels.

The general was busily engaged with his secretary at the moment of their entry, so that for a brief space Jack was at leisure to study his surroundings. He was quick to seize the opportunity. Observation with him was an instinct derived from the strain of aboriginal blood inherited from his great-grandparents. The instinct had been further sharpened by the training of his boyhood in the open, and confirmed a little later on by his occupation as a kangaroo hunter. Lastly, his experiences of the desert warfare, during the past two years or so, had developed his great powers to such an extent that he was able at a glance to take in the details as well as the broader outlines of a landscape or any other place with unerring accuracy. As a proof of the quality of his quickened powers, he carried in his mind a photograph, so to speak, of every inch of the way travelled from the time of his capture by the Bedouins, as well as the contour of the whole countryside that came within the range of his eyesight. He could re-travel the tortuous and rugged, often pathless, way at any moment, without making a fault.

The general presently looked up from a large section map which he had been scrutinising, and from which his secretary was making extensive notes at his dictation. He returned the salute of the captain and gave a pleasant nod of recognition to Jack. He then turned to his secretary and spoke a few low words to him. The official thereupon promptly gathered up the plan and his notes, and, after rolling them up with others of like nature, placed them upon a high shelf which stood in one corner of the room. He then left the room, passing through another door than the one by which the others had entered.

The moment they were alone the general bade the captain draw up two chairs close to the table and sit down. While the captain was bringing the chairs together, Jack looked intently into the face of the chief. While his features were true to the Tartar type, they were not so heavy as the general run of his kind. Nor were his eyes accompanied by the sinister expression so quickly detected by the Western eye. There was something about this sparely-built, alert-looking, elderly general which was very acceptable to Jack. He felt that, whatever might be the outcome of the interview, he would be justly, if not kindly, treated. This is not to say that he could look upon this man as a friend, and go easy in his presence. Anything but that. While his eyes were not so crafty as those of the average Turk, there was a shrewdness and alertness which boded ill for anyone questioned by him, should he seek to evade the questions by the ordinary tricks of the dissembler.

The first question put Jack perfectly at ease.

"So you are the great British general whom friend Yacob has so fully described," said he, with a quizzical smile, as soon as they were seated. "To be frank, you are a very far remove from the great Bluebeard who led the army of the terrible Giaours against our puny forces in the desert. Had I believed all the Arab said about your person and reputation, I should have looked for a human tiger of the man-eating breed, whereas—"

"You see before you a specimen of that common or garden variety of the Britisher, who appropriately bears the name of Smith," promptly interjected Jack, while the ghost of a smile quivered the corners of his mouth.

"Now, that's not at all bad," retorted the general, with a quiet chuckle. "'Smith' sums up the situation in a syllable. If, in addition to that, your parents by any manner of chance prefixed the name 'John,' your identification would be made absolute."

"In a moment of inspiration, derived from the fact that my father and grandfather, and doubtless countless Smiths in order of descent before them, bore the same name, I was duly and solemnly christened 'John.' But I'm bound to say that the effect of this has been marred to some extent by my family and friends, who persist in calling me 'Jack.'"

"'Jack'? Why, man, that has been your salvation. There's a whole hemisphere of difference between 'Jack Smith' and 'John Smith.' 'John' Smith predicates the very undesirable quality of portentous dullness. It stands for orthodoxy. It is reminiscent of cold plum-pudding. On the other hand, 'Jack' Smith—well, a Jack might become anything from a gay pierrot up to a Prime Minister! Yes, by the Great Horn Spoon, that's a cinch!"

To say that Jack was surprised at the general's speech is to describe his feelings mildly. He was quite taken aback for the moment. It was quite plain that this man's personality could not be summed up in a syllable. His humour, certainly, did not bear the Eastern brand. It was distinctly American. Was he, after all, a Turk? Might he not be a renegade Englishman? Or an American? But no! His features, despite certain modifications, were decidedly Eastern.

"I see you are trying to place me," continued the general, as he marked the puzzled frown on Jack's face. "Let me solve the riddle. I was a military *attaché* to the Turkish legation at Washington many years ago, and—"

"Enough said," broke in Jack. "That accounts for the traces of Uncle Sam in your phrases."

"Well, now, Mr. Smith, I'm going to ask you a question. What is your rank?"

"Major, sir."

"Good! Did you join on a commission? You're so young-looking, you know."

"No, sir. I joined as a full private."

"Ah! That decidedly spells merit. I congratulate you."

"This is queer stuff he's serving out," thought Jack. "Wonder what's at the back of his words?"

"Where did you enlist, may I ask?"

The general's single question was multiplying into many. Jack hesitated a moment. Where was he being led to? Still, no harm could come from a knowledge of his nationality. It couldn't be guessed, of course, from his uniform, which had become reduced to rags. Anyhow, he would be close the moment the questioning reached danger point.

"At Brisbane, Queensland, Australia."

"Australia! Why, then, you're an—an—Anzac?"

"In the literal sense, General. I had the honour of meeting your brave countrymen on Gallipoli."

"No troops in the world could have performed more brilliantly," said the general gravely. "Yet you never saw Constantinople."

"That's true enough, General. We're looking towards

Jerusalem, however, for compensation."

The general gazed steadily at the young Anzac for a few moments. Then he spoke quietly, but with the accent of conviction.

"Your hope for Jerusalem is a vainer one than that for Stamboul. Your troops are now menacing Gaza. Let me tell you this: your great Gibraltar is not more impregnable than Gaza. You beat us in the desert, it is true. But after our first attack on the Canal, which failed because we were too far from our base, we did not take the desert fighting seriously. We fought rather to delay you until we had completed our plans for the defence of Palestine. Now we are ready for any eventuality. No, no, no! Your chances of seeing Jerusalem, save under our escort, are less than a million to one."

"A million to one?" repeated Jack, with a smile, "It certainly isn't very encouraging, is it?"

"Ah, well, a truce to predictions for the present," laughed the general. "You will be with us for a while. Will you take parole?"

"That would rob my mates of the fun of rescuing me."

"So it would. A pity to block such a laudable undertaking. Until such time as your friends see fit to convey you back in an aeroplane, we'll treat you as decently as circumstances permit. Are you quite comfortable?"

"Everything's perfectly dinkum, General."

"You're beginning to think the Turkish devil is not quite so black as he is painted, eh?"

"If not dazzlingly white, he is anything but black, judging from our experiences," replied Jack, with a merry laugh. "I should be inclined to paint him a light grey."

"We'll let it go at that, Major. Now I come to think of it, you could do with some decent clothes."

"That's true. Especially underclothes. And, if you could add a razor for—"

"You shall have it. Captain, take Major Smith and also his sergeant to the photographer for identification purposes, and see to it that they have everything they require in the way of clothes."

This, with a nod, indicated their dismissal.

If the general designed to puzzle Jack, he succeeded remarkably well: it was altogether so different from what he had expected. As far as he could judge there was no hidden motive in the general's mind. It was the sort of talk that any well-disposed persons might indulge in when coming together for the first time. There did not appear to be any intention, either by question or suggestion, to draw out a piece of information which would be of importance to the enemy. He finally concluded that the present interview was to be regarded as a mere skirmish. The next would be more advanced in its nature. How this proved the first and last encounter between the two will be told in the next chapter.

CHAPTER X

HOW JACK AND JOCK DONNED THE TURKISH UNI-FORM

"WELL, I'll be everlastingly blest!"

These words of astonishment came from M'Thirst, who at Jack's instance opened the bulky parcel of clothing which arrived at the hut within half an hour of their return from the photographer. They were told to return to this functionary for another sitting as soon as they had shaved and redressed themselves. The Turks were evidently determined to make their identification sure, whatever happened.

"What's up, Sergeant?" exclaimed Jack from the doorway.

He was at this moment intently watching the movements of a small group of mounted Bedouins who were skirting the trench system with a view to entering the camp. The main entry, it should be said, was made by bridging the trenches at a certain spot. A beaten road led through the entanglements on the far side and across the portable bridges. A strong guard, in addition, was posted, and admission was gained only by the talisman of a password.

"Hold on a moment," continued he, his eyes following the moving group as they neared the entrance.

Why should Jack be so concerned about this small party of nomads? They were only one of numbers of similar groups of this class in the employ of the Turks, for similar purposes. They were continually coming and going. Yet this bunch, as like any other as peas in a pod, turned his casual glance into an intent and searching gaze. Although a full third of a mile distant, his keen eyes had detected a familiar figure among them. As their progress across his line of vision brought them a little nearer, the recognition became clearer. He had now no doubt as to the identity of the object of his close scrutiny. His convictions were confirmed by a further recognition of the animal which the person in question bestrode. The camel was curiously marked. The marks had often been noticed and commented upon by those familiar with these beasts, and this second identification brought the utmost satisfaction to the gazer.

"Drop that drapery, Jock! Come here quickly!" cried he in excited tones to his mate.

"Yes, Major; what's the trouble?" said M'Thirst, when he stood at the other's side.

"D'ye see that bunch of Bedouins yonder?"

"See 'em all right."

"Recognise any of 'em?"

"Can't say I do," replied Jock, as he strained his eyes.

"Focus your peepers on that tall chap, third from the front."

"Yes, I spot him." -

"Know him?"

"Know him? No—o—o. Hanged if I do!"

"Know the beast he's riding?"

"Why—a—let's see. It does look a bit familiar. Seems as if I'd seen it before. I'll be blest, though, if I can remember where!"

"Just fancy your not knowing an old friend when he comes to visit you!"

"An old friend? Cut it out, Mister Jack. I ain't got no friend among these vermin."

"Well, who owned the beast which you once described by saying that it carried the map of Queensland on its off side?"

"Why—a—a—a!" stuttered Jock, as a flash of recollection seized him. "You don't mean to say yon's your old friend—Eid?"

"I do mean to say it, and say it deliberately."

"But—er—er—all these Bedouins are as alike as a mob of Chinamen."

"It's beyond all argument, Jock. If we were as sure of escape as I am certain that yonder chap's Eid—!"

"I believe you, Major," said M'Thirst, after a prolonged stare. "I recognise the old rascal. Wonder what he's here for?"

"He's tracked us, of course."

"Rubbish, man!"

"True as gospel, Jock."

"But—er—!"

"But me no buts. It's not at all surprising to me. Mackenzie and Tim Hogan, to say nothing of our colonel and the others, would not allow the matter of our disappearance to grow cold. They are sure to exhaust all means of finding our whereabouts. And this is one. Take my tip; Eid's been on the job. I'd bet a mountain to a molehill that Jock Mac and Tim are behind this. Trust our old pals for that."

"You're right, Major," said M'Thirst, with quiet emphasis. "At the same time, it's not beyond the old chap to do it on his own. Begum, you're the one white man in the world for the sheikh. All the same, I believe it's a concoction. The boys have put their heads together, and sent him on the trail. You can gamble on the old sheikh for nosing us out all right."

"That you may. He's as keen as mustard on a scent. First cousin to a bush black."

"Wonder how he got to know we were here?"

"That's as plain as pie. Old Yacob's brought him here."

"Old Yacob? Why, where does he come in?"

"You silly clown!" broke in Jack, with a ringing laugh. "Why, he's riding at this moment at the head of his mob. Don't you spot him?"

"Well, if I'm not the two ends of a double-dyed duffer! Of course I recognise him an' the whole bunch now."

By this time the Bedouins had reached the main entrance, and after challenge by the guard, passed through, wheeling in a direction which took them farther away from the hut. Presently they disappeared behind the horse-lines.

"How'll we get in touch with 'em, Major?"

"Trust Eid to do that."

Jack had no manner of doubt that the old sheikh had located them, and was contriving a way of escape.

But who is this Eid? A word of explanation to the reader is necessary here. A true and abiding friendship had sprung up between the sheikh and Jack during the first months of the desert campaign. It commenced with the never-to-be-forgotten patrol to the Maghara Hills to locate an enemy stronghold. On that occasion Eid was guide and scout. Owing to an accident, the leader of the squadron was placed *hors de combat*, and the command devolved on Lieutenant Smith, as he then was. During the attack on the oasis, which was an exciting incident enough, Jack and Eid saw qualities in each other which begot a mutual respect that further adventures only served to heighten. This ripened into a friendship as rare as it was unusual. On Eid's side it took the form of a devotion which lasted through the campaign. The two were thrown much together through being picked out to do special observation work. It was in this way that Jack acquired a good working knowledge of Arabic, which often stood him in good stead.

A feeling of great contentment came over him when he knew that his old desert friend was at hand. Once in touch with each other it would go hard if they could not devise a plan which would quickly bring freedom.

"Let's go in now and inspect this wonderful parcel, Jock. What was it that caused you to give that yell of astonishment when you untied the bundle?"

"See for yourself," was the laconic reply.

"And these are the contents!" cried he a moment later. "By Jupiter! A pair of brand-new razors, a strop, shirts, underpants—and socks, by all that's heavenly! Toilet soap, linen handkerchiefs! If I ever! After this, Sergeant M'Thirst —the millennium!"

"You can call it what you like," rejoined his companion with scorn, as he held aloft a soldier's tunic. "But I call it what it is—a dirty Jacko's uniform!"

"Ah-ha!" shouted Jack, as he exploded in a laugh. "No, no! That's hardly the symbol of the millennium. As a matter of fact, it's both clean and new, but, of course, one would never dream of exhibiting a Turk's tunic at the masthead as the emblem of universal peace."

"The Dagoes! Like their bloomin' cheek! To load this muck on to us! Fancy me in a Johnny's duds—I don't think! Here goes!" cried M'Thirst, as he seized the two uniforms and flung them into the fireplace. "Where's a match? I'll send 'em to blazes before you can say knife!"

"You'll do no such thing, you thundering ass!" shouted Jack, as he rushed to the fireplace and retrieved the uniforms ere Jock could commit his act of arson. "Can't you see, you juggins, that these uniforms are the very things above all others that we need at the present moment? Why, man, they're a regular godsend! I had a plan in my head to visit the men's lines at night and pinch a couple of their suits. It's a necessary disguise. And you to go and throw these—! By the tailor of Mars, it's getting down on your marrow bones you ought to be in sheer thankfulness!"

Although Jock's guns were silenced, his resentful feelings remained. That the hated uniforms were to be viewed as instruments of salvation in no wise abated his prejudices. "I'll be everlastingly frizzled if I stick my legs in a bloomin' Turk's breeks!" muttered he mutinously while Jack was examining the garments.

"I say, Jock," remarked the other when he had completed his survey of the uniforms, "the beggars have sent us suits corresponding to our rank in the army. Don't take it too hard, old fellow. I'm not in love with 'em myself, you bet. At the same time, we must stoop to conquer, you know."

Jack had an irresistible way with him. Although Mac

did not weaken in his aversion to the Turkish garments, he was prepared to swallow the dose, and follow his major's lead in anything that would win them freedom.

In less than an hour the two Anzacs had shaved and donned their new clothes. Jack observed with secret amusement that Jock bestowed sundry kicks upon the unoffending trousers ere sticking his legs into them.

The transformation was marked. By Jack's design both had shaved themselves in the fashion affected by the Turkish military, the result being that they would easily pass muster in the dusk of the evening as Mussulman soldiers.

"I suppose, sir, we'll have to go back to the blessed photographer and be taken in this rig?"

"Not on your life! They'll have to send for us if they want us. I don't think that old chap'll give us a second thought. The captain, you know, said he had to return to his batt. So we'll play 'possum on that proposition. After lunch I'm going to get in touch with Eid, if possible. It will be a test of this disguise at the same time."

"Disguise? I guess you'd pass muster at midday among them chaps. You're tanned as brown as a berry to start with; then the clothes fit yer like a glove. Besides, the way you manage yer eyes, to say nothin' of yer strut. Oh! you'd fool 'em all the time."

"Righto. I think I'll just fade away."

"Ain't I ter go with yer?"

"No, old fellow. Stick to the hut, keeping your eye skinned, of course."

"You'll not do anything rash, Major?"

"I'm not going to run much risk. I want to avoid awakening suspicion. But, as you know, it is necessary to get into immediate touch with Eid. I thought at first I'd let him make the first move, but I now have a feeling that it would be easier for it to come from me."

So complete was Jack's resemblance to a Turkish officer that nothing but a close and critical inspection would reveal the truth of his nationality. He was determined to trade boldly upon this disguise. He felt that time was the essence of the contract, and that to proceed straight to his object was the wisest plan. To loiter about in the role of a Turkish officer would be to awaken suspicion.

The camp, it must not be forgotten, was small in area. A small body of mixed troops, including artillery, comprised its garrison. Its remoteness from the enemy lines, and its proximity to one of the main camps of reserves, made a larger force unnecessary; while, on the other hand, the absence of the bustle of a large camp rendered the work of Headquarters more congenial.

On leaving the hut, Jack walked briskly to the main buildings, crossed the front, and then altered his course till he faced the rear of the camp. By this it would appear to any whom he might meet that he was coming straight from the general's quarters. This supposition would naturally include the surmise that he was carrying out a military duty. One thing to specially guard against was that of being held in conversation by a Turkish officer. That undesirable *recontre* avoided, he felt confident of success.

The old adage held: Fortune favoured the brave. While crossing to the rear of the camp, which abutted the railway line—and where he was sure the Bedouins were located—he encountered several soldiers on foot, and a troop of cavalry which was proceeding on some errand. Luckily, he did not meet any Staff officer. Acknowledging the salutes of the men as they passed, he held on his way across the camp and along the infantry lines. There, in a far corner, between the infantry and cavalry lines, he discerned a couple of black tents, and knew them for those of the Bedouins.

Many eyes followed him as he passed through the lines on his way. But in the glances of the sprawling soldiers there was naught of suspicion. They were simply glances of idle curiosity. If his brisk movements prompted any remark at all, it was that of sneering surprise that any fool officer should so dissipate his energy in the sweltering heat of the afternoon.

The Bedouins were, for the most part, lying under the shade of a clump of bushy trees: Two of their number were issuing from one of the tents at the moment Jack reached them. He knew them at the first glance. They were Yacob and Eid. They, on their part, saw only a Turk in an officer's uniform. For a few seconds they stood in perfect silence, face to face.

Eid was not often startled out of that condition of impassivity which was habitual to him, but the unexpected words, and still more the action of this smart, smiling Turkish officer, did the trick.

"Eid, old friend," warmly exclaimed Jack, breaking the silence as he extended his hand in a friendly handshake. "It's good for sore eyes to see you again."

"What!" continued he laughingly, as he saw the startled look on the old man's face, followed by a puzzled frown. "Am I then so soon forgotten? What about the Maghara Hills?"

It was worth something to Jack to see the change in the sheikh's countenance as his reference to the famous exploit to the Meghara Hills brought back to him a flood of recollection and recognition. There was no mistaking the shining face and the look of glad surprise, nor was there any lack of warmth in the handgrip which instinctively followed.

CHAPTER XI

HOW JACK PLANNED AN ESCAPE

"ALL ready, Jock?"

"Ready."

"Lower that light a bit, will you? No! That's too much. Ah! That's better! Mustn't let 'em think there's anything unusual up. Yet if we don't dull the light, it'll show us up as we cross its beam. Keep low down. There's too much starlight for us to take any liberties."

The two men had stolen quietly from the hut through the back doorway. Half-stooping and half-crawling, they progressed through the darkness, worming themselves along the dusty ground as they crossed the faint beams of light which issued from the window. In this noiseless advance they shaped their course in the direction of Headquarters. They could have wished for a starless night to assist them in the adventure they were now undertaking. Brilliancy is a distinguishing feature of the Syrian skies. Even the Australians, whose own southern skies are radiantly beautiful at night time, had to admit the brighter lustre of these star-spangled heavens. Their silvery beams seemed to make a mockery of the darkness.

Such conditions made their advance doubly difficult, yet they were equal to the occasion. By hugging the earth as closely as possible without actually crawling, they made swift advance. They had almost reached the shadows cast by the main building when the first danger assailed them.

Jack Smith was priding himself upon the complete success of their adventure so far, when the sound of rapidly-advancing footsteps, making in their direction, became audible to his ears.

"Hist! Flatten yourself!" was all that he had time to whisper to his comrade, when a squad of men rounded the comer of the building and marched along its side.

Had they been a little nearer the building the fugitives could not have escaped discovery. As it was; the squad passed within twenty short feet of them. By good fortune nothing happened. The soldiers, a picket, passed on their way in ignorance of their presence. Had the Turks, however, been looking around with suspicious eyes, they would have quickly discerned these log-like objects. But Johnny Turk has one thing in common with Billjim Anzac. He has thoughts only for the tucker bag. Like all others of their class the returning squad, making a bee-line for their billet, had all their thoughts focused upon the cook pots.

"Say, Mac," whispered Jack, as soon as the retreating footsteps of the soldiers became faint, "that was a near go! We shall probably meet other similar parties. Better to stand up. We'll kid 'em that we're one of themselves."

So saying, both men rose to their feet and advanced towards the wall, ready to run the gauntlet of detection, on demand.

When Jack and Eid met in the afternoon it took but a few minutes to make the position clear. Eid, as the youths had surmised, had been engaged by Jack's old friends, Mackenzie and Hogan, to endeavour, by penetrating the Turkish lines, to discover the whereabouts of the missing men. To this undertaking they gained the colonel's approval; and Eid himself was more than willing to start upon this adventure. It was not the money promise that incited him. He was, of course, in a general way as avaricious as the average Bedouin, who thinks no risk too great if there is profit to be made; but in this case it was a genuine affection for the young Australian officer that was his motive. For his sake he was willing to run the gauntlet of death.

Eid's native shrewdness, together with his knowledge of the country and the freemasonry which existed between the clans, combined to make his quest a success.

Although some weeks had elapsed ere he set out, he was soon able to get an inkling of the state of affairs. His principal difficulty at the beginning was in dodging the Turks, who were doubly alert after the Battle of Rafa; for the British menace had now developed its strength in Palestine. They had lost no time in following up their successes on the northern border of Sinai. Within a few days of the capitulation of Rafa, advanced bodies of Light Horse were in the vicinity of the ancient capital city of Philistia, Gaza. The advanced scouting parties were quickly followed by solid bodies of troops, travelling by sea and land, until in a short time strong pressure had been brought to bear upon the venerable but well-fortified city.

This rendered a great Turkish concentration necessary, and the whole countryside east and north of Gaza became a scene of marching columns of enemy troops. Eid's one fear was that he might be recognised by some Turkish officer or soldier. The double part he had played at Maghara Hills would ensure a short shrift once he was identified.

Unhasting and yet unresting, he wormed his way through the hostile sections. Picking up information at every available place and piecing it together with the practised skill of a Sherlock Holmes, no sleuth ever held more tenaciously and unwearyingly to the track of his quarry than Eid to his single purpose—the locating and liberating of his friend.

At length, when he had got behind the Turkish main lines, he received some definite information. This started him on the straight trail. It so happened that he reached Yacob's headquarters, if a nomad's collection of tents and huts could be so designated, on the night of the escape of the lads from the surveillance of the clan. Eid claimed kinship with Yacob's lot, and was welcomed by the greatly perturbed Bedouins, whose excitement at the escape of the prisoners had developed into hysteria.

Within a few hours of Eid's arrival, Yacob and his men

appeared upon the scene. The humour of the disgruntled sheikh may be better imagined than described. Every Turk, whether in heaven or on earth, was cursed with a thoroughness and fluency which left nothing further to be desired, from the standpoint of evil intent. Eblis, the prince of Mohammedan devils, was adjured to practise all his refinements of torture, in particular, upon the immediate frustrators of the sheikh's cherished designs. He called for the very direst calamities to descend upon the heads of the patrol officer and his general for their conscienceless breaking of the agreement, upon what he considered an absurd technicality. In a word, he cursed himself into an epileptic fit.

This, fortunately for all, was of short duration, and upon his recovery, Eid, in a few words, made it abundantly clear to his cupidity that all was not lost. Let him but follow the other's lead; render the service desired; and a talent of silver would immediately become his prized possession. Thus would he achieve two desirable results: he would be revenged upon the Turks, and at the same time become a wealthy man.

A single dose of this medicine shrewdly administered by Eid completely cured Yacob's megrims. A vision of shining silver formed an effectual anodyne to his lacerated feelings, while the prospect of sweet revenge acted as a stimulant to his vindictive desires. Hence the subsequent appearance of the two chiefs at Headquarters. Not all of Yacob's retinue entered the compound. Some of his men, with two spare camels, lay within a couple of miles, securely hidden in a dry donga amid the hills. Thus far had Eid schemed for the liberation of his friend. So far so good. But of course the main problem was that of getting the two youths safely through the camp barriers. He had no cut-and-dried scheme for this part of the proceedings. The scheming for this would be the task of his friend Jack. Of Jack's ability to concoct a workable plan he had no more doubt than of his own existence. His experience of

Jack's resourcefulness in the past placed his competency beyond all question.

It did not take the two friends many minutes to agree upon a plan when they met. What Jack said went with Eid. Two things had added greatly to their chances of escape: first, their comparative freedom, and then the uniforms. It would go hard if they failed to break camp under the present conditions.

Jack's plan was the essence of simplicity: they would simply walk out. All the machinery required was a password, and the getting of that devolved upon the two sheikhs.

The captain's threat of a bastinado, should he ever be caught lurking about Headquarters, did not greatly alarm old Yacob. He looked upon the threat as harmless so long as he made no demand upon the general for compensation. He had been used, time and again, by the Turks for spying purposes, and was sure that his entry would not excite any opposition. It was different with Eid. He ran a risk of being recognised. He was, so to speak, putting his head in the lion's mouth, yet for friendship's sake he was ready to violate his cautionary instincts.

Just before sunset Yacob approached the hut, and passed by without look or word. Jack, who was looking for something like this, watched him through the window curtains. He saw what he expected. A tiny scrap of paper fell to the ground.

He made no immediate effort to retrieve this, but later on, when the dusk deepened, he sauntered towards the spot. There was only one word on the paper. It was the password.

The Bedouins departed at nightfall. The prisoners were to make their escape at the earliest moment. Although there was much in their favour, there was none the less need for care. A curiously-minded guard might ask questions that would excite suspicion. Still, with a little bit more of luck, there was a good sporting chance of winning free.

But something remained to be done before the gauntlet of the barrier was run. Ever since the interview of the morning an idea had been taking root in Jack's mind. Why go empty-handed? What about that roll of plans which lay on the high shelf in the general's sanctum! What wouldn't the British Headquarters Staff give for a knowledge of their contents! It would be a prize worth winning.

The more he thought about the matter the more deeply was he convinced that it was his duty to seize them if possible.

The chance was too good to be let slip. It is doubtful, however, if he would have succeeded in his intention but for an unexpected occurrence which, until it came, was outside his knowledge and, therefore, his calculations.

He had conceived a plan of purloining the documents. The main window of the general's room was on the side which faced the prison hut. Once within the room he would make short work of the business. He was counting on its being empty, for the attempt would he made during the dinner hour, when the Staff were dining in a distant part of the building.

When he stood before the window he found that, by a stroke of good luck, the sash, though lowered, had not been fastened. He quickly, yet noiselessly, lifted it to its full height. A faint light gleamed through the darkness. The tiny point of flame scarcely prevailed against the dark. It was enough, however, for Jack's purposes. Leaving M'Thirst to keep watch and give the alarm should it be necessary, he entered through the window, and crept to the shelf in the corner whereon the roll lay. It did not take many seconds for him to untie the roll and distribute the plans and other matter about his person. He also pocketed a revolver which lay on the centre table.

His errand was now accomplished. He grinned at the thought of the easiness of the job. The whole proceedings had taken barely two minutes. It seemed too good to be true. Should his luck continue, they would be free men in a very short time.

Lingering not a moment longer than was necessary, and remembering the need of caution, and the more so that things were going so well, he sidled past the long table, on his way to the window. Suddenly he stood stock-still. Every limb in his body stiffened as he stood at attention. His keen ear detected a noise which came from the corridor. A hand was fumbling at the knob of the door which gave entrance from the passage. The next second it was flung wide open, and an officer, apparently in a hurry, stepped into the room. Striding to the table, he turned up the wick of the lamp, whose strong light now filled every part.

Meanwhile Jack had been prompt to act. The moment he heard the turning of the door-handle he sank to the ground and slid under the table. Had the visitor delayed his arrival for twenty seconds or so, the intruder would have made his exit.

What should he do now? To be caught red-handed could have only one conclusion. The amiable, well-disposed general of the morning would become the stern, pitiless executioner of the night. He would order him to be shot with no more compunction than if he were a pariah of the gutter.

Jack was under no delusion. His attempt to escape, if frustrated, might be condoned, but the theft of important military plans during wartime was a crime of the highest magnitude, to be rewarded with a bullet through heart or brain, with the alternative of the hangman's rope. But Jack did not mean to be caught if he could help it. For one thing he had a loaded revolver; then the other man was ignorant of his presence. Should he be discovered he would have all the advantage of surprise. Not that he wanted it to come to a scuffle. If the Turk, whoever he was, would take his departure, he—Jack—would be well content.

But that was just what the man in question had no intention of doing. He had come for something that should be in the room. Was it the revolver? It could not have been the plans. Were they missed from their place, he would make an immediate outcry. Whatever it was, it was worth being looked for. His rapid search was accompanied with maledictions, which, had they materialised, would have frizzled the offending article to nothingness.

"P'raps it's under the table. I must look."

"Phew!" breathed Jack. "Now for it! The Cross versus the Crescent!"

With his eyes fixed on the legs of the Turk as he bent over to seize the lamp from the centre of the table, the concealed youth gathered himself together so that he might make a sudden spring when the searcher peered beneath the table.

The man was in the act of lifting the lamp when he suddenly replaced it, and stood a moment in a listening attitude. At the same moment there came to Jack's ears a peculiar droning sound, which grew louder and louder as the seconds sped, accompanied now by a rattling noise to which the drone acted as a background. There was no mistaking the sounds. They meant the swift advance of an aeroplane. Friend or enemy—which? The same thought occurred to each mind.

The doubt was settled in an unquestionable manner. The anti-aircraft guns had got to work with commendable swiftness.

At the first sound of the guns the Turk bolted through the door and up the corridor. Jack lost no time in getting out of the window. He had scarcely reached his companion when a loud explosion shook the earth. This was immediately followed by the crash of falling ceilings and walls. The building just vacated by him had been struck in that portion occupied by the offices.

The two youths stood, dazed by the suddenness of the occurrence.

CHAPTER XII

HOW JACK STOLE THE PLANS, AND HOW THEY WON FREE FROM TURKISH HEADQUARTERS

ANYONE who has seen a hawk swoop down on a covey of feeding quail will guess the effect produced in the Turkish camp when the British aeroplane hovered over it with hostile intent. The nimble quail in seeking cover from the predatory foe scarcely excelled in expedition the helter-skelter rush of the Turks. But whereas the birds run from the open into the stubble at the flash of the hawk's wings, the soldiers, on the contrary, rushed from cover to the open spaces.

The greatest danger in their case lay in crumbling walls and falling ceilings. A building, unless bomb-proof, might easily become a death-trap.

The wildest confusion now reigned. It was heightened in a few minutes when sounds from the aeroplane indicated its return. By a quick order all lights were extinguished, and the camp was plunged in darkness.

The prisoners no longer had any fear of detection. It seemed as if the very heavens had conspired in their favour. They were sure that not a thought would be bestowed on them while the scare was on. Here, then, was the chance of a million.

"If I only had my old squadron," thought Jack, as they walked with a quick stride towards the bridge, stumbling occasionally over the prostrate forms of frightened soldiers, "I'd have this blessed garrison on toast in ten minutes."

Not a solitary guard was to be seen, and no one challenged them when they reached the bridge. The strong picket had scattered far and wide.

The situation was so grotesque that for the life of them the Australians could not help breaking out into loud laughter, despite the risk of being discovered. But for that moment they were quite safe, for the Turks had ears only for one thing—the sounds of the returning aeroplane. All other sounds were meaningless to their seared minds. The lads' laughter, if heard, would be simply regarded as maniacal.

"Farewell, Johnny!" shouted Jack from the far end of the bridge. "And if for ever, still, fare thee well!"

"Now then, Jock, old man," cried he, the next moment. "Old Eid'll be wondering whether we've been blown up. Listen! There goes another bomb. By Christopher! Hear 'em yelling?"

"Begum, Mister Jack, it's funnier than a circus. Who'd have dreamed such a thing could have happened?"

"A comic opera's not in it, Jock. The boys'll never believe our yarn. The whole thing, ever since we entered the camp, has been farcical to a degree. Hanged if I can straighten it out, anyway. It is absolutely idiotic. It is nothing to our credit, let me tell you, that we're careering over this track unpursued. The veriest dunderheads could have skipped as easily. Talk of the stars in their courses fighting against Sisera! Seems to me our stars have been fighting for us all through. Ah! Here's the branch track. We follow this."

They were now about a mile from the camp. Under the prevailing conditions and the exhilaration consequent upon their easy exit from the Turkish stronghold, they had for the moment abandoned the caution which had hitherto characterised them. They were soon to learn that it is not well to holloa until one is well out of the wood. They had not travelled a hundred yards along the branch track before they ran into a patrol party that was returning to camp. The horsemen were going at a rapid pace in open order, covering a wide face. They were too near to be evaded. So there was nothing for it but to take one's courage in both hands and command all one's wits.

Should the patrol halt to question the travellers, whom they could not fail to see in the bright starlight, Jack did not feel too sure of being able to bluff them. They might ask awkward questions; Despite the Turkish uniform they wore, suspicion might easily arise through their speech. While largely based on Arabic, the Turkish is a composite language. A chance word might give them away.

Jack, however, made up his mind like a shot. Before the advancing patrol could draw rein he sang out loudly some words of command that he knew were familiar to them: "Camp's attacked! Gallop! General's orders!"

Hearing this order lustily given in peremptory terms, and not doubting for a moment that it was given by one of their own officers, the patrol immediately quickened its stride, and swept onward at full gallop. It was with difficulty that the lads escaped from being overridden by the rear files.

Ten minutes later they met Eid at the spot agreed upon, who piloted them to the rendezvous. He had heard the rattle of the aeroplane and the bomb explosions, and made a pretty shrewd guess at the condition of things. He was confident that the incident would be to the furtherance rather than to the hindrance of Jack's plans.

There was no thought, however, of taking things easy. The main thing was to get going and to travel as far as possible from the vicinity before daylight. Things at the camp would be sure to be in confusion for a while, but order would, sooner or later, be restored. It would not be long before the theft of the plans would be discovered; the prisoners remembered; the hut visited; and then would the heather be set on fire. The telephones would get going, and in a short time search-parties would be scouring the country in all directions.

The boys wished that the Turks could be kept in ignorance of their accomplices. Nothing, so far as they were aware, connected the Bedouins with their escape. No one had seen through Jack's disguise when he visited the sheikhs in the camp. These nomads came and went as suited themselves, and their leaving before sunset created no curiosity, nor called for any remark. It was a great thing to have these fellows as friends. They could be trusted—at any rate Eid could, and Jack would no more think of doubting his friendship than he would his own father's word. Yacob, of course, stood on another plane. He was not under the obligation of friendship. The only bond between him and the young Anzacs was a cash tie. On the other hand, his relation to Eid was one of blood. Eid had an ascendancy, and what he said was law with Yacob. Under these conditions the latter could be relied upon. Even M'Thirst, who had no liking for Bedouins in general, and the utmost contempt for Yacob in particular, had no qualms in following their lead.

Not many minutes elapsed after the arrival of the lads before the party moved out from the donga and took a direction under the guidance of Yacob, who knew every inch of the country. The guide took the line of least resistance. That meant that the course was anything but straight or direct.

Many outposts and garrisons were scattered through the country, to say nothing of the lines which would have to be pierced before winning through to the British positions.

Yacob's task, under all the circumstances, was anything but an easy one. The old man, however, did not lack faith in himself. Jack had nothing but admiration for the clever manner in which he twisted and turned, yet never at a loss for direction, and always true to the main course. These détours, seemingly meaningless at times, were always justified—twinkling lights seen from high points, or dark forms moving in the uncertain light of the stars, acting as warnings to the guides.

The party apprehended little danger from pursuit. The course taken by Yacob would baffle much quicker-witted trackers than the Turks. Still, they were passing through hostile country thickly strewn with posts and mobile forces. In addition to this, and unknown to them, the whole countryside had been put into motion for their capture. Headquarters was in touch with all the smaller garrisons of its military district. To these peremptory orders were issued within an hour of the escape. The general's first thought after the explosion, which worked havoc with the main building, was the rescue of his plans and papers. As soon as he reduced the chaos which ruled throughout the camp to some form of order, he organised a fatigue party to remove the debris from his room. It was not long before he discovered the loss of his papers.

Who had committed this crime? The papers had not been destroyed by the explosion. Of that he felt sure. Fragments would surely be found. The most diligent search, however, failed to unearth a scrap. There was only one alternative to destruction—theft! But by whom? It was at this moment that his mind reverted to the prisoners. Were they the culprits? If so...!

A rapid order was as rapidly executed. The men returned in a few minutes empty-handed. The birds had flown. The general was not much surprised at this. He had come to a swift conclusion. The prisoners, taking immediate advantage of the confusion created by the bomb-throwing, had decamped, carrying with them a set of plans and other papers which would be more precious than rubies to the British. Yes, that was it. How they had done it he could not for the life of him understand, but that his surmise was correct he had not the slightest doubt. There was only one thing to be done: the fugitives must be recaptured.

To this end the whole countryside was set in motion. The fact was made known that two Australians were at large somewhere in the military area, making for the British lines, and patrols were sent out to scour in every direction. Reward and promotion were offered to anyone who should capture them, and the direst penalties were threatened against any who should let them slip through their fingers.

That some such scheme had been set afoot became

evident to the fugitives as the night wore on. Yacob, shortly after the start from the donga, sent some of his men forward on foot. These scouted around and ahead, giving warning from time to time of the near approach of hostile bands. Before long it became clear that small bodies of Turks were acting in concert. It was only by keeping clear of all beaten tracks that they avoided collision.

"Look here!" exclaimed Jack to the sheikhs, after they had narrowly escaped contact with a small detachment of Turkish horsemen. "The old general's alarmed the district. Anyone with half an eye can see that. They're on the search all right. Daylight'll soon be here, and what will our chances be then? Do you know of any place where we might hide during the day?"

The old men agreed in the seriousness of the situation. It did certainly look as if the whole place was being traversed by search-parties. Advance under these altered conditions made capture almost certain, were they to press forward in the daytime. Concealment was their only course. Did Yacob know of a spot where they would be effectually screened from the most inquisitive eye? Yacob could lead them to such a place. There was such a spot in the hills, well known to roving Bedouins, but quite unknown to the Turks—unless, indeed, they had stumbled upon it during some recent movement.

Action waited closely upon resolve. No sooner had they determined upon this course than they begun to retrace their steps. Turning sharply to the left at a certain point, they speeded along a dry watercourse. Should nothing occur to hinder, Yacob was sure of reaching the hiding-place before daybreak. Nothing but praise could be given for the skill shown by the old Bedouin in guiding the party over the difficult country and evading the hostile bands. Yet, despite all the intimate knowledge, wonderful instincts, and resource possessed by the Bedouins, they were shortly to receive a check that would upset all their well-thought schemes.

They were threading the bed of a winding wady in

Indian file. The watercourse at this point ran through precipitous cliffs, becoming a mountain torrent in the wet season. The country all around was broken into rocky hills and deep defiles. It was sterile and wild in character, and was uninhabited. It looked an ideal place for hiding.

Suddenly, as thus they moved forward and upward to their covert in the heart of the hills, there came down on them a small body of horsemen. It occurred just at the moment when the Bedouins believed themselves to be beyond the danger zone. They had called in the men who were scouting in the front, and in a few minutes would reach on ana-branch, short in length, which ended in a cul-de-sac formed by a series of caverns. These were big enough to hide a company ten times as large as that now seeking sanctuary. The two parties came together as each was rounding a sharp curve, in opposite directions. There was no time to do anything. Escape was impossible. They simply ran into one another. No side could claim a monopoly of surprise. For some moments Turk and Bedouin swayed and wrestled in the utmost confusion.

By a great stroke of fortune the young Aussies were riding towards the rear. The battle now was to the quickest witted. Before the jostling ended Jack had acted. He sensed the trouble in a flash, and knew what would inevitably follow did he not take immediate notion. For one brief second he encouraged the desire to bluff. Could he not pose as a Turkish officer leading a band of Arabs in hot-foot pursuit? The thought was instantaneously dismissed. It was bound to break down. His speech would betray him.

There was only one trick left. Flight!

"Slip off, Jock," whispered he to his mate.

"It's our only chance to get clear of this melee."

This was no sooner uttered than acted upon. Slipping to the ground they worked their way, with much squeezing, through the struggling camels. The moment they won clear they sprinted along the sandy bed at the top of their speed.

CHAPTER XIII

HOW THE AUSSIES RODE INTO A TURKISH
PATROL, AND WHAT CAME OF IT

IT is pretty safe to say that Jack's thoughts sped even faster than his feet. His hard thinking eclipsed his hard running, and presently controlled his swift movements to such an extent as to reduce them to a slow trot.

This gait was not at all to M'Thirst's liking. He was for giving no chances. Already to his excited imagination the Turkish horsemen were clattering down the track in hot pursuit.

"What's the matter?" cried he, when the other slackened his pace. "Not blown, are you? They'll be on top of us in a shake unless we keep goin' full pelt."

"Listen!" said Jack, pulling up to a dead halt. "I've been figuring it out. We're running right into danger. The farther we go the worse it'll be for us. We'll probably smash into another lot. Oh, there's no danger at present! We're jolly lucky to get out of this pickle so easily. Those beggars haven't got out of their tangle yet. When they do straighten out, their officer'll take a good ten minutes in exhausting his vocabulary of expletives. I'm dead certain no Turk sighted us.

Trust old Yacob to give a plausible explanation of their presence as soon as they get a chance to chip in."

"But what about our camels? Won't they—?"

"I can hear the old sheikh explaining the thing as sweetly and smoothly as a purring pussy. He had heard about the escape of the British prisoners, and had been told to take a hand. He had consequently joined in the chase, and was even now combing out likely places. The riderless camels? That was easy to explain. They were to bring in the infidels when they had run them to earth."

"We know the old Dago's a daisy at lying; but the thing is, what are we going to do?"

"Do? Going back."

"Goin' back? Why, you must be stark, staring mad. It's not me as'll go hack. You'll go alone this time."

"No, I won't. You'll come with me."

"What? Right into their jaws?"

"Sergeant Jock M'Thirst!—Attention!"

Mac instinctively straightened out and stiffened himself in the correct attitude.

"Right turn!"

Without a second's hesitation the non-com turned in the required direction, which brought him facing the steep bank of the wady.

"March!"

The next moment Jock was scrambling up the almost perpendicular bank in the rear of his commander.

When the two had reached the top of the high, steep bank in a somewhat breathless condition, M'Thirst began to realise that his major was not quite so mad as he appeared to be a short minute ago.

"I—I—thought you meant going back up the trap."

"And of course wrote me down as a fool, eh?"

"Well—a—"

"Oh, it's all right. Now we'll get along."

"It's this way, Jock," said he, a minute or two later, after they had struggled through the mass of brushwood which grew thickly upon a sandy ridge. "It's no use our going down the wady. Our plan is to hide up here somewhere till dusk, and make a bold bid to get through to-night. But, first of all, I want to find out what's happening yonder."

Making their way up the left bank of the wady, but far enough away to be invisible to any curious eye, the lads, despite the rough travelling, soon arrived at a spot opposite to the bend of the watercourse where the two parties rode into one another. The high-pitched voice of the Turkish captain could be distinctly heard before they had crept in to the brink of the bank. Looking down, after a cautious advance to a shrubby spot on the edge, they had a clear view of the parties underneath. It was evident that they had come to some understanding. Exactly what it was they could not, at the first, comprehend. The action of the Turks, however soon dispelled any doubts as to what had taken place. It was simply this: the captain had commandeered the Bedouins. He was keen on arresting the runaways. Spoils and promotion to the victor! As the sheikh knew every nook and corner of the hill country, his presence was invaluable; so without any more ado, he and his ragged retainers were laid hold of and used as hounds in the capture of the very youths whom, up to this moment, they were pledged to save.

Scarcely had they sensed the altered relation of their friends when the troops were in motion. The cavalcade, to their joy, proceeded down the wady. Night was now merging into day, and their movements were followed with intentness as they passed through the paling shadows of the wady's bed. For some reason or other the Bedouins had been distributed. One section was placed in the lead, while the remainder made up the tail of the force.

Jack's first thought was for Eid. He was certain that his friend had not lost his head in the confused jostle of the forces; that all through the scrimmage, while men's tongues and even fists were actively employed, he had thoughts only for the main chance. Eid, he was sure, would be the first to miss them. He would understand all right. Trust the subtle Ishmaelite for not being more than a thousand miles from the truth! It was therefore with great satisfaction he noticed his friend, upon the disposition of the Bedouins, manoeuvring for a position at the rear of the column.

As a matter of fact, Eid, who at the beginning of the confused struggle had been well in the front, began to edge towards the rear. He had no wish to come in contact with the officer. Backing his camel adroitly, he wormed his way, stem first, through Turk and Bedouin, until he found himself in the rear. The sight of the two riderless camels did not surprise him. Surprise would have been felt had it been otherwise. His friend, he was sure, would not be caught napping. He had skipped at the first contact. They were not the fellows, however, to yield to panic. They were somewhere in the vicinity, no doubt, and were interested spectators of the mix-up.

He had no more intention of following the Turks than had the boys of being captured. This determination was founded upon two reasons. The first we know. It was the inviolate bond of friendship. Please Allah, it would not be long before he rejoined his friend. The second reason, though less strong, was his fear of recognition. He knew they had marked him down for the part he had played in Maghara Hills, when he led Jack's squadron on that famous reconnaissance. And now, to his dismay, he recognised the Turkish captain by his voice as the man who had acted as interpreter on that eventful occasion. It was far from his desire to stir up unpleasant memories by thrusting himself upon the notice of the captain. To such a contingency he could only anticipate one ending—the lodgement of a bullet in a vital part of his anatomy.

It was, therefore, with an appreciable amount of satisfaction that the sheikh took up the position of last joint in the tail of the column. As they proceeded down the wady he kept both eyes and ears on the alert for any sight or sound that would indicate the whereabouts of his young friends. He was not kept long in suspense.

"Come along, Jock," said Jack, as soon as the Turks had got in motion; "we'll follow 'em up. Must get in touch with Eid somehow. See how the cute old beggar's tailing up. Take my word for it, before they've gone very far something'll happen to his camel or saddlery that'll give him a chance to lag behind."

"He's not too bad for a Dago."

All foreigners were Dagoes to M'Thirst: Gypsies, Turks, Arabs, Bedouins—even French and Germans—were all comprehended in that one word.

He was the most conservative of Britons in his racial prejudices. No one troubled himself less in matters touching the internal economy of the British Empire, yet to none did he yield in his belief of its right and power to lead the world.

Jack gave a smile of tolerance at the expression. Jock was a Jew of the olden time. All who were not Jews were Gentiles, and, therefore, quite outside the charmed circle.

"I'll lay a slice of mother's cake to the grubbiest biscuit in the commissariat that the shiekh'll do as I said!"

"Begum, you're right enough, Major!" exclaimed his companion, after they had followed up the column for half a mile or so. "See! He's dropped his rifle. Good on the old man!"

Waiting his opportunity, which came while the force was rounding a sharp turn, he allowed his rifle to fall with a clatter on the stones. Halting his steed, which he made to be a slow process, he leisurely slid to the ground and walked at an equally slow gait to where his weapon lay on the gravel. By this time the whole column had disappeared round the corner.

But instead of picking up his rifle, Eid cast his eyes upward, rapidly scanning both banks. He was not kept long without a sign. A cap was thrust out from between some bushes growing at the edge of the bank almost opposite him. No more was needed. His shrewd surmises had materialised to a nicety.

After a moment's exposure the cap was withdrawn, and Jack's head cautiously protruded in its place. He was taking no risks. Speech was not essential to communication between these two. Before he had become sufficiently proficient in Arabic to converse in that language, he and Eid had developed a sign-language by which they were able to understand each other in all that related to the ordinary things of life. At the present moment they instinctively fell back on their system of ideagrams. This was compounded of the Australian aboriginal sign-language, in which Jack was fairly proficient; that used by the Arabs, in which Eid was

"Jack's head cautiously protruded."

skilled; together with certain military flag-signals.

They came to a perfect agreement, through the use of this sign-language, regarding their plan of procedure. The lads were to make for the place of concealment indicated by Yacob. At the proper time Eid would slip away and rejoin them at the caves. This simple arrangement having been made in less time than it takes to tell it, the Bedouin picked up his rifle, and then, without taking any further notice of the lads, remounted his camel, and was soon out of sight.

"What's to do now, Major?" said M'Thirst, as soon as the sheikh had disappeared.

"We're to proceed to the caves as originally intended. Eid will levant at the first fitting opportunity and meet us there."

Jack had not the slightest doubt about finding the hiding-place. Striking off at a tangent from the wady bank they struggled through the difficult country adjacent to the watercourse. Not-withstanding the *détours* that were necessary in order to make any sort of progress, the line of direction was followed. After proceeding in this way for an hour or so they reached the bank of the ana-branch, some distance back from its confluence with the main wady.

It will be remembered that this tributary ended in a cul-de-sac formed by a precipitous range of hills, at the base of which was a series of caverns. This was reached in due time. Here they were to await the arrival of Eid with what patience they possessed. They were foodless, but, luckily, a deep pool at the branch-head provided them with cool, sweet water.

The lads, after a little exploration, came to the conclusion that there was nothing intricate in the caves. They did not extend far in, being for the most part cavernous holes in the side of the declivity. These were independent of each other for the most part. The one, however, which they selected opened out into an inner room, which in turn connected with a third that had an outlet in the face of the cliff. The selection of this suite provided them with a way of retreat should it be necessary.

"I say, Mac," exclaimed Jack, when they had scrutinised the caves, "this set of rooms will suit us down to the ground. Tell you what: we'll gather a couple of bundles of bracken out yonder, and cart 'em into the inside cave. Then we'll indulge in what my eyes have been asking for ever since sun-up—a dreamless sleep in a comfy bed."

"What about watch an' watch?"

"Don't think there's the slightest need for it. I seem to have a feeling of absolute safety. The risk's too trifling to worry about."

If the major, who was generally so keen to provide against contingencies, saw nothing to worry about, M'Thirst was sure that he wasn't going to store up any. There were only two things worth worrying about. He was as hungry as Esau, and as sleepy as Dickens's fat boy, Joe. The craving of hunger would have to remain unsatisfied for a while, but they could sleep at any rate. Once in the land of forgetfulness, the pangs of hunger would cease from troubling.

It was well in the afternoon when Eid arrived on the scene. After locating the lads, he shook them into consciousness. His presence more than compensated for the rude awakening. It was a proof that things were not so bad as they might be. In addition, and what was of greater moment just then, it meant a feed. The Bedouin had not come with empty pockets. Venison and barley bread, when there's plenty of it, is good enough for any hungry lad.

The sheikh put them in possession of the facts of his adventures in a few words. After going down the wady for some distance they abandoned it, and followed a road which led through a long, fertile valley, in the centre of which was a Jewish village. The village was deserted.

Let it be said by way of parenthesis that about this time the Governor-General, Djemal Pasha, issued an ukase by which the Jews were being driven out of Palestine. Their ill-concealed joy at the prospect of the entry of the British forces stirred the ire of the Turkish authorities, and furnished Djemal Pasha with an excuse for their deportation. Thousands had already been banished from Jaffa, Jerusalem, and other places, and their houses pillaged and looted by Turkish soldiers and Bedouins. The Governor-General, it is true, stopped short of cold-blooded massacre. Yet his calculated policy of starvation and deportation was designed to the same end. This is not to say that there were no violent murders. There were very many. The roads to the north that were lined with refugees were the scenes of appalling cases of cruelty and robbery, accompanied by death at the hands of banditti hordes.

The village at which the Turkish search-party halted was a case in point. It had been recently deserted. There was food in plenty, and, in addition, most of the Jewish goods and chattels were left behind, for the refugees were not allowed to take more than they could carry on their persons.

The temptation to loot was too great in the present instance for the Turks and Bedouins to withstand, even though they were engaged on special service. A bird in the hand was worth two in the bush. The looting business had this advantage for Eid: it furnished him with a splendid opportunity for escape. As soon as the party had satisfied their hunger, they proceeded to go through the houses in a systematic manner. In this congenial work Yacob and his merry men played no second fiddle.

Eid was the one exception. Hastily collecting a quantity of food, together with some male garments which he found in a house not yet looted, he proceeded to where the Turks had stacked their rifles. From the pile he selected two weapons and a goodly supply of ammunition. With them he retreated to where the camels were camped, and in a few minutes had secured them to his saddle. With due caution he led his beast back to the outskirts where they had entered the village. From there he travelled at a forced march, arriving at the rendezvous at the time related.

"My word, Eid, old friend. you have done splendidly. Tucker, guns, clothes! It's dinkum all right. I'd been wondering how we could get rid of these Turkish togs. The Jackoes, of course, have been posted up about our uniforms. These'll help to put 'em off the scent. If you'd only thought to bring back our camels!"

"No good. We'll do better on foot for the present. Later on, with luck, we'll have horses."

"Meaning?"

"If we can win through to a certain place, my friends will supply the horses."

"Good! I'll feel twice the man with a piece of good horse-flesh between my knees. You're right, too, about the camels. Now, Eid, you get to bye-bye. Jock and I have had a sleep. You must be dead tired, old fellow, and a long night's before us, with no easy programme to carry out."

CHAPTER XIV

HOW THE TURKS SET A TRAP, AND
THE RESULT

DAY was dissolving into night when the escapees left their retreat and entered upon the task of threading the way through the foothills on the road that led to liberty. The word "road" must be taken in a very broad sense, for, literally speaking, roads there were none. Narrow paths, it is true, zigzagged among the gullies and hills at intervals, criss-crossing one another, and leading everywhere and nowhere. These were made by sheep and goats, especially the latter, in their wanderings during dry seasons in search of the scant pastures of the highlands.

Roads, however, of whatever kind, were not for these men. They were things to be avoided. Owing to what had happened on the previous night, they were obliged to modify their plans The separation of Yacob and his tribe made a change imperative. The hazard of breaking through the Turkish lines in the vicinity of Gaza, without the help of the Bedouins who alone could guide them through the intricacies, was too great to be practicable.

After conning the situation they agreed that it would be much better to proceed in a roundabout fashion. The longest way round, in this case, would be the shortest way home.

On leaving the caves they bore in a south-westerly direction. Had they been able to pursue a straight line of travel they could have reached their present objective in a few hours' walk. Once there, they would be out of the hill country and in possession of the horses which Eid had arranged for with his friends. They would then strike due south till they reached the southern border. From that point they would make west for Rafa, which remained in the hands of the British, and thence the journey along the military route north to Gaza would be a mere picnic.

They were not unmindful that the plan they purposed following might have to be modified in some directions —might even have to be abandoned. The night, too, operated against fast journeying. But for all this their spirits rose exultantly. The joy of adventure was upon them. They were confident of winning through against all odds, and it would go hard if they did not get through to Eid's friends by sunrise. After that, with decent animals under them, they would make it a steeplechase to the border.

But though they proceeded with vaulting spirits, their confidence did not lead them to rashness. They set their course by the stars, and though the deviations were many owing to the rugged nature of the ground, and later on as they entered a settled district long *détours* had to be made in skirting villages and farms, yet on the whole they made better progress than they had expected. Their fears had not been for the villagers but for lurking Turkish soldiers and those in their employ. The peasants would be more likely to aid than to hinder them. Still, they regarded, and wisely, every settlement as a danger zone because of possible Turkish occupation.

They had to halt or retreat several times during the night because of the movements of troops. On one occasion they were almost caught, and had to beat a rapid retreat, owing to the quick movement of a party of horsemen on a slope down which they were travelling. The slope was bare of any cover, and the starlight was too brilliant for them to take any risks. The Turks were advancing in open order, and were too near for the lads to manoeuvre out of their path. There was nothing for it but to cut and run. In this they had to accommodate themselves to the sheikh's pace. His years were against fast travel for any considerable distance, especially uphill. The horsemen were gaining on them, and Eid, with the best intentions, was weakening in his stride. They were yet some distance from the crown of the ridge, which was covered with thick bushes, and at the present rate of going the enemy would catch them before they could reach cover. Jack, however, was equal to the emergency. As soon as he became sensible of the sheikh's lagging footsteps, and found that he was nearly spent, he called to his mate, who was some little distance ahead. Then ranging himself alongside, he seized an arm, while Jock laid hold of the other. Half-dragging, half-carrying the old man, they quickened their pace to a final burst, gaining the shelter of the scrub scarce one hundred yards in advance of the Turks.

Fortunately the latter slowed down upon reaching the scrubby ground. This enabled the fugitives to dodge among the bushes until they were well on the flank of the advancing men.

"Begum, we just managed to beat the favourite this time, Major!" exclaimed M'Thirst in breathless accents as soon as the Turks had trotted past.

"'Twas too near a shave to be pleasant, Jock. Besides, the sheikh's all out."

The tremendous spurt uphill, added to the long hours of rough walking in the dark, touched the limit of the old man's endurance. He lay awhile on the ground in a crumpled-up condition, blowing like the proverbial grampus.

He rallied sufficiently, however, after a short time, to make a start. Every moment was precious. Owing to many *détours* and this set-back, they were still a considerable distance from the place where the horses were located. Day, too, was fast approaching. For all that there was not any great cause for alarm. Unless they were greatly hampered in their progress they would make the rendezvous before dawn. The sheikh, whose tottering footsteps, when they left cover, gave rise to apprehension, soon got into his usual stride. His spare form had the quality of whalebone, and was well under the control of his inflexible will.

The trio travelled for a full hour with scarce an interruption. They passed what appeared to be a large body of troops, keeping well on their right. Camp fires gleamed over a large area of land. While they paused a few moments in silent gaze the réveillé sounded.

"The beggars are standing to. They've got all their cook pots going. Looks as if they were going on a stunt."

Jack's surmise was correct. Though he was unaware of it, they formed a body of reinforcements going post-haste to Gaza to strengthen the garrison which was on the eve of being attacked by the British.

Continuing their way unmolested, they reached an area of broken country on the edge of the maritime plains, which constitute the coast region. It was in the midst of this cluster of hills that the horses to be supplied by the Bedouins were awaiting them.

The sheikh was now on familiar ground. He led his companions without any hesitation through a twisting gully to one of the natural fortresses which abound in Palestine. Here a few determined men could hold off a brigade. The gully merged into a deep canyon scarce fifteen feet wide.

This formed the inlet to the rendezvous. Here Eid was to meet his friends, who, at a favourable time, were to guide the party by unfrequented ways till well to the south.

Although there was no reason to believe that danger lurked within the area, the trio did not forget that they were still in the woods, and that time was not yet to halloo. They were not taking any undue risks. True, as Eid remarked just before entering the hilly maze, had the enemy shown any sign of his presence, warning would have been given ere passing into the area. The absence of any friendly scout as they entered the defile was reassuring. Yet instinct sent out its warnings, and these may never be ignored with impunity.

A deep, brooding silence enveloped them as they proceeded along the winding gully. It gave the feeling that they were shut out for ever from the rest of the world. The silence itself was uncanny: it was too intense. It pervaded Jack's sensibility and quickened his pulse. For the first time throughout this adventurous night-tramp, he felt a chill sensation that was not caused by the temperature. The whole of the surroundings seemed unusual. There was no rustle of vegetation; no sound of falling or running water; no scuttle of creeping reptile, or of any kind of bird or beast; no sough of wind or earth noises such as are common to the experience of travellers. Their cautious footsteps on the soft sandy bed made no echo. The new day that was spreading itself over the outside world had not yet begun to modify the interior darkness of the region through which they were moving. There was nothing, in short, in their present surroundings to indicate the presence of any beings save themselves.

But it was this very combination which gave rise to a strong feeling, both in Eid and Jack, and to a lesser degree in M'Thirst, that things were not altogether what they seemed. This feeling deepened as they proceeded, until at last, to Jack at least, it became a threat. Without uttering a word, each member of the little party eased down to dead slow. At the same time their faculties reached a pitch of alertness, which became an almost intolerable strain. Yet what was there to be alarmed at? Should not the very darkness be taken as an assurance?

They had now reached the point where the gully raised its walls perpendicularly until it assumed the proportions of a canyon. In a very few minutes now, even at their present gait, they would enter the level area, flanked by precipitous walls, where the Bedouins were waiting with the horses.

Suddenly, as thus they advanced through the canyon with soundless tread, a piece of rock fell from immediately above them, rattling down the uneven walls, and striking the earth just behind them with a thud. The noise of the falling stone, had it been in the daylight, and under ordinary circumstances, would hardly have excited notice, but in the present situation its effect was electrical. Each man stood in his tracks, while he peered around and overhead. The sound, however natural, became ominous. But it was what followed that gave colour to the apprehensions of the party. Scarcely had the falling stone struck the ground when another sound reached Jack's ears. It was a sibilant note of warning. Focusing his keen eyes on the spot from which the sound issued, he detected a shadowy form, which presently dissolved in the darkness, as though retreating from an exposed position on the brow. The suspicion had now become a certainty. A trap had been set. They were calmly entering its mouth.

Now arose a question: had they been detected? Jack quickly came to the conclusion that the Turks were aware of their presence, and were about to close the trap. They had already travelled two-thirds of the length of the canyon. A short distance now would bring them into the fortress.

What was the best thing to do? It was at this point of momentary hesitation that light came upon the situation —not from within but from without. With startling suddenness the area above and below was lighted up with a brilliance which made every object to stand out clearly. Jack, whose head was at the moment upturned, detected the cause in a flash. A Turk was standing on the brink overhead holding a large flare in his hands. But he hardly stood for five seconds in this attitude before it slipped from his nerveless grasp to the ground. His body swayed and tottered on the edge of the precipice, and then fell forward and downward to the bottom, while the reverberations of a rifle-shot echoed through the hills. These had hardly ceased before they were multiplied thirtyfold by the fusillade of the Turkish soldiery, aimed at the spot where the momentary flare revealed the sheikh and his companions. By the time the Turks lining the sides of the canyon near its mouth had emptied their magazines by continuous fire, the men below must have been riddled with bullets—supposing them to be still there. But to the chagrin of the soldiers, when another flare cast its beams downward, the expected sight of crumpled-up, lifeless bodies was denied them. There was one lifeless body, it was true. It was that of their leader.

CHAPTER XV

AN AEROPLANE TO THE RESCUE

STEADY, Jock. 'Member Eid. Mustn't wind the old chap. Aren't the Jackoes burning powder! We should be killed a hundred times over."

"We didn't skip a moment too soon, begum! Didn't take 'em long to get busy with their shootin' irons. But where are we to head to? Keep along this track?"

"Eid'll give us the lead. He knows this place. Said a moment ago there was a good place farther on. Wouldn't do to go too far along this gully. Bet a dollar we were spotted when we entered and the way out's blocked."

Jack's surmise was correct. They had been betrayed. Yacob and his men had given them away. It came about in this fashion. One of the sheikh's retainers, in a moment of confidence, had bragged about the plot to a Turk, and this man, as soon as he had wormed the plan from the boastful Bedouin, took the news to his captain, who acted promptly. The sheikh was summoned to his presence, and confessed to the plot under the pressure of torture. But while he admitted being a party to the scheme for getting the British soldiers back to their friends, he remained silent over Eid's share in the transaction. That stood for grace to him. He was true to the bonds of kinship. Nor must he be over-blamed for his confession, or for his statement of the plan relating to the execution of the plot. His service to the Anzacs rested on a purely commercial basis. Besides, he had not recovered from the bitterness of his chagrin at their escape from his hands when he held them for ransom. Lastly, there was the threat of a bastinado, plus fanciful markings with hot irons. Horrible visions of what might be in store for him overcame any remaining scruples.

The captain was not slow to turn his information to good account. His first intention was to proceed to the eaves where the fugitives were supposed to be in hiding. But second thoughts determined him otherwise. They would probably have left their retreat, and it would be quite easy to miss them. Better by far to hurry to the rendezvous and await them there.

He worked out his plan and set his trap with commendable cleverness. He left some of his men near the entrance to the hill section, after instructing them to scout over the country through which the fleeing men would be bound to travel. Once they entered the defile there would be no getting out. The men on guard at the entrance would see to that. After fixing a field-telephone receiver at a convenient place, he ran the line along the bank of the gully as he advanced. Thus would his men outside be enabled to apprise him of the exact moment of the party's arrival. Then, when he had surprised the horse-holders at the rendezvous, he stationed his men at the point of the inlet, on both sides of the canyon.

The plan was cunningly designed and cleverly executed up to a point. The Turks were fairly stunned for some moments when they realised the blow dealt them by the fatal rifle-shot. It was not until the second flare lit up the place that they became aware of the tragedy. They had no intention, however, of allowing their quarry to escape. The moment the lieutenant saw the body of his captain lying on the sands beneath, he took up the leadership, and signalised it by ordering an immediate start in pursuit. But before leaving he telephoned orders to the men at the outlet. Not many minutes passed before the troopers had vaulted to their saddles and issued from the rendezvous in quick pursuit. Daylight was beginning to make itself felt as they clattered down the wady.

"This way," said Eid, after they had been going at a round pace for about half a mile. "Follow me."

Suiting the action to the word, he clambered up the bank at a point where a hog-back ridge intersected the gully. The ridge had a steep gradient for some distance back, when it abruptly inclined toward the horizontal for a little space, and then rose almost sheer till it junctioned with a flat-crowned hill. This hill was peculiar in shape, its walls inclining outwards in many places.

Accepting Eid's leadership, the boys followed him without a word. As Jack surveyed the hill before him he felt it was hardly the place he would have selected, as there seemed to be no way of retreat should they be driven to attempt it. But then, thought he, it's the best place known to Eid or he would not bring us to it.

They had now advanced to the stiffest part of the climb, and one that taxed their utmost efforts. They could not afford to slacken, for they might be discovered at any moment. The darkness had vanished, and in the pearl-grey light of the dawn they stood revealed to any curious eye.

It so happened there was one very curious eye among the pursuing Turks. It belonged to the lieutenant. He was not at all sure that the pursued would stick to the wady. As they galloped along its bed he eagerly scanned both sides for signs. Nor was he long without his reward. Suddenly pulling his horse to a standstill, after crying a halt, he examined some marks on the left bank. Tumbling from his horse he followed the tracks which led up the ridge. Casting his eyes upwards to the hill beyond, he gave a vigorous view-halloo.

"Come on quickly!" shouted he. "We've got them. See the rascals—one, two, three, climbing the hillside! They shall not escape us this time."

Clambering up the gully bank, the horsemen forced the pace up the ridge until they could get no farther, owing to its precipitous nature. By this time the fugitives, by almost superhuman efforts, were nearing the summit. Jumping from their steeds the Turks let drive at them. It was resultless, however, for in a few seconds they gained the crest and disappeared.

"By gum, we just beat 'em!" exclaimed M'Thirst in gasps, as he threw himself on the ground. "The bullets from those snipers were coming too close to be pleasant. Crikey, look here! Blest if one of 'em hasn't taken off the heel of my boot. Thought I felt a jar. It'll cost a bob or two to have a new heel put on."

"Be thankful it's only a heel of your boot and not the heel of your foot. My word, Eid, we can defy a squadron here!"

The Turks proved determined foes, but the attempt to carry the position by a *tour de force* was easily defeated by the expert riflemen. After a vain endeavour to ascend the scarp, during which they sustained several casualties, they retired to cover. The attempt convinced them that with their present numbers it was impossible to take the position by main force; but there were other ways. One was to strongly reinforce their numbers.

Another and less expensive way was to starve the defenders out. The summary measure found general acceptance, and a messenger was forth-with sent at speed to the nearest outpost. The men were then stationed in positions where it would be impossible for the prisoners to attempt escape without being observed.

The youths were not unmindful of these dispositions. They were able, from their coign of vantage, to follow all the movements below. They could not but see that time was against them. They had, it was true, some fragments of food remaining, and were used to going for long periods without food or water. Ah! Had they only water they could hang out for days. That, more than food, was a necessity. The very thought of it, even in the cool of the morning, created a thirst. There was another essential factor—ammunition. Their supply was limited to a few clips.

So the day wore on. Early in the afternoon the watchers in the heights observed a column of dust on the horizon. It was a sign of marching troops. Later on they distinguished a body of horse- and camel-men moving at a fast pace in their direction. They were the reinforcements. In an hour or so they would effect a junction with the men at the foot of the hill. These, so far, were ignorant of their approach. Jack laid no flattering unction to his soul over the evident importance attached to his capture. He was perfectly sensible that the zeal of the enemy was due mainly to the important plans he was carrying, the placing of which in the hands of the British would amount to a disaster. They must be retrieved at all costs.

It was within an hour of sunset that the column reached the vicinity, to the unbounded delight of the others. In comparison to the strength of the foe to be dislodged from the heights it made a formidable array, amounting to about three troops. A hundred men to capture three, who had scarce a dozen rounds of ammunition apiece!

It did not take the newcomers long to make their dispositions. They intended making an attack simultaneously from three points. The men stationed at the far side of the hill during the interval of awaiting reinforcements had discovered what they considered two accessible tracks. This would split up the parties and make the assault a mere bagatelle. So rightly reasoned the Turkish colonel who was in charge.

It cannot be said that the lads viewed these preparations with equanimity. They knew perfectly well that unless something unexpected happened in their favour they were done. Had they an unlimited supply of ammunition they would have a good sporting chance of holding back any rush. But as things were, there was not much to count upon. Still, they did not despair. They would make it as hard as possible for the other side.

Jock and Eid were to guard the main position, and Jack was to cruise along the brow at the rear to pop off adventurous climbers who might scale the heights by the back-stairs. As he thus coasted the brow he suddenly stood stock-still, straining his ears. Yes; there was no mistaking that droning sound—an aeroplane.

Looking sharply upwards he detected a tiny speck coming out of the east—high up, momentarily growing larger. Was it friend or enemy?

While he stood intently watching the approach of the 'plane, a fusillade from below broke the stillness. The Turks were putting up a barrage, under cover of which the storm-troops essayed the scarp-climb. This was something the defenders had not counted on. They could do nothing against such tactics. Any exposure meant death or serious wounds. The only chance left them was to deal with the attackers as they reached the brow.

The troops had just begun the climb, when Jack gave a loud cooee. Turning at the sound, the others beheld him pointing towards the sky. Not able to leave their post, they, like Jack, divided their attention between the enemy and the aeroplane.

Presently the machine dipped, and then came on at a low level. Jack could now detect the occupants. Throwing down his rifle he extended his arms in wild gesticulation, muttering the while, "If it's an enemy they'll be none the wiser; if one of our own, they'll know."

"Hurrah! Hurrah! It's one of our own!" The signal had been answered.

The aeroplane was now circling overhead, and soon spotted the attacking Turks. The tables were immediately turned. A couple of bombs, well delivered, filled them with a wild panic. The next moment the survivors were rushing down the slope, pell-mell.

CHAPTER XVI

HOW THE EUREKA AMALGAMATEDS
CELEBRATED JACK'S RETURN

"BEGORRA! but 'tis graate news ye've told me, Liftinint. Eid's on the thracks of the byes? They're in the hands of the Jackoes? Way back in the hills of Judee? Praise the good Lord for that!"

"Tim, Tim! I'm astonished. Praising the Lord for the captivity of your best pal, to say nothing of poor old Jock M'Thirst! Last thing I'd 'a' expected from you."

"Look here, Jock Mackenzie, if ye weren't me suparior officer I'd be callin' ye names that'd reflect severely on yer intilligence. Didn't ye be afther sayin' only yisterday that if Jackie wor above the daisies we'd 'a' heerd from him weeks ago? Makin' me that miserable wid yer blessed pissimism that I dhramed last night I saw him lyin' in his windin' shaate. An' now ye're chiackin' me for me natcheral expression of thanks to the Almighty at the graate news that he's still alive an'—!"

"Well, old man, if you put it that way I withdraw any remark calculated to wound your tender feelings. Joking aside, I was that elated at the word the young Bedouin brought me, one of Eid's men, y' know, that I grabbed his hand with forty-horse-power, and would have fallen on his neck in true Eastern style but for the scared look on the beggar's face. He seemed to think I'd gone dilly. The colonel, who was standing by, was quite sure for the moment I'd got a touch of the sun. I'm with you in thanks, old man. Trust Jack and old Eid to slip out of any noose the jolly Jackoes might throw round 'em!"

"Bedad, thin, ye're quite right. There's not a Turkey prison made that'll howld the Sanior Partner wance he an'

Eid gits a whisper together. But how'd the man what towld ye git to know?"

"That's more than I can tell you, Tim. These fellows have ways of communicating, something like the 'bush telegraph' over in our country, in the old days of bushranging. This man had been out on the right flank, and came in touch with another joker. It came along that way by word of mouth."

"Faix, thin, but I whisht the dear man was wid us at this moment, so I do. It's out of the fun he'll be intoirely. P'raps he'll turn up in time."

"You can hardly put a limit to old Jack. Anyone who knows him as we do 'll back him any day in the week to do the possible. But nothing less than a miracle 'd land him here in time."

"Who's that magging about the limit, and the possible, and declaring against miracles in the Land of Miracles?"

At the same moment the tent-flap was thrown back, and Jack Smith, clean-shaved, and dressed in a spick-and-span uniform, stood in the opening, his arms akimbo, his brown cheeks flushed, his eyes snapping sparks of joy, his whole face lit up in a merry humour. Thus he stood in the framework of the doorway before his old pals, enjoying to the full their speechless amazement.

"By Samson Agonistes!"

"Be Saint Jawn of Jerusalem!"

"Jack!"

"The Sanior Partner of the Yewrekas!"

"Is it you or only your jolly ghost?"

"Let me touch you wid me little finger to prove that you're on'y flesh an' blood," cried Tim Hogan, as he launched his wiry frame upon the upstanding figure in the doorway. The next moment the three "marsupials" were in the throes of a wrestling match. Had the Chief looked in on this tussle between two officers in uniform and a stretcher-bearer, he would have frowned to some purpose, despite his knowledge of the free-and-easy manners of the Australians. Happily this particular scrimmage, indicative of the mutual delight of the Australian lads, which ignored for the moment all distinction of rank, was beyond his ken.

After a few moments' jostling, the living, palpitating knot of humanity separated itself from the serum in its respective persons. Their breathless condition typified the unspeakable happiness which the safe return of their comrade created.

"Jackie, me darlint, till me, arre ye none the worse for yer adventures?"

"He looks weak and ill, Tim, I don't think. What makes you ask such a fool question of the fellow who came off top-dog in the scrum? My word, Jack, you're still as tough as an old-man kangaroo!"

"Don't waste any sympathy over me, Tim. I'm as right as rain and as fit as a fiddle. If I *were* feeling a bit off, the sight of you two would work an immediate cure."

"But, Masther Jack, wud ye be afther tillin' us where ye came from, an' where owld Jock M'Thirst is?"

"From Headquarters, sonny. Jock's doing what I hope to be losing myself in as soon as I can tear myself away from your company."

"An' what's that?"

"An able-bodied sleep."

"Now thin, Masther Jack, none of yer shinanegan. From Headquarters, ses ye, an'—"

"Quite correct. Had to report to the colonel. He dragged me straight to the Chief, who put me through my facings. From there, when I'd cleaned up, I made a bee-line here and had the luck to find the two of you in close confab and argument over the ancient proposition, are miracles possible?"

"Look here, you old prodigal, if you don't give a sane answer to Tim's question, *instanter*, and tell us *how* you got back from the Never-Never, that we'd just heard through one of Eid's men you'd been taken to, we'll—well, we'll do something dreadful to you."

"'Eadquarters is all right, Masther Jack, but till us how ye came acrost the Turkeys' lines!"

"Flew."

"Flew? Ye'll sure be tillin' us next that ye sailed home in an aeroplane."

"Well, s'pose I did say it? What then?"

"Aw, nothin'. I'd simply hand ye the firrst prize widout a moment's hisatation."

"What—for lying?"

"No, no. Nothin' like that. Just for a flight of imagination. 'Romancin',' I wance heard our major call it."

"I see. How do you take it, Jock?"

"Don't want to be rude, old man."

"All right. I see you're a pair of doubting Thomases. If nothing but absolute proof'll satisfy you, I can soon furnish you with that. But in the meantime I'll give you the whole rigmarole in a few sentences."

At that he related his experiences with the Bedouins and Turks, concluding with their sensational rescue by the aeroplane, at the moment of their recapture.

"There now, red-head. D'you believe me now?" said Jack, with a broad grin, when he had finished.

"From hinceforward an' for ever."

"But it's been M'Thirst this, and M'Thirst that, all through the piece," broke in Mackenzie.

"What I want to know is where Jack Smith comes in?"

"Get out. I've poked myself in quite enough. Let me tell you, chaps, old Mac's 18-carat gold."

"Tim and I are not finding any fault with the Bobnawarra champion; he's all right. Wait till I cross his track. Bet you my Sunday boots his version'll give a different colour to the business, old man. But, I say! what price the stacks of letters that have come for you! I'll get them this moment from my bag. Of course you'll send a wire to your people immediately?"

"They've got it by this time," was Jack's smiling reply.

Jack's luck was in. He was in time to rejoin his unit and take his share in the hard fighting in the British offensive, which began two days later. His reception by his Chief and the members of the Staff was most cordial in its nature.

And it can easily be imagined how quickly the news of his escape from captivity and return would spread through the camp. The plans and other documents supplied information of the greatest importance, and later on when Allenby's great drive began, the data thus supplied were of material service. The modest yet graphic account of his experiences heightened the already brilliant reputation which he had achieved for daring exploits during me Sinai campaign. In this recital both M'Thirst and Eid got their full meed of praise.

Eid, it should be said, did not return to the British lines. When the aeroplane landed on the flat-topped hill to pick them up, the Bedouin refused to budge. This was in part due to a natural fear of the aeroplane, which was an exceedingly uncanny thing to his sight; but principally to his desire to recover his camel, to which he was strongly attached, and his determination to find out the cause of the betrayal. To do this he would have to get in touch with Yacob. That accomplished, he might be trusted to adopt those subtle desert tactics for probing the matter and eventually meting out revenge to the guilty parties. As to the risks of his remaining in the enemy country, they were small when he had only himself to think of and care for. There was no immediate danger from the Turks. The aeroplane bombs had frightened the wits out of the attackers, whose one thought was to escape pursuit. So, despite Jack's entreaty, the old sheikh remained. This was to bear fruit after many days, as will be seen later on.

CHAPTER XVII

HOW THE BRITISH FAILED TO TAKE GAZA

THE attack upon the Turkish fortress of Gaza differed in many respects from the desert fighting which preceded it. The decisive battle of El Romani, when 20,000 Turks were handsomely whipped, with 9000 casualties to the enemy, was fought in the open, and won mainly by the Light Horse and Yeomanry, whose mobile forces broke up their formations and confused their strategy. This great blow was followed up without pause, and El Arish, Maghdaba, and Rafa fell in rapid succession. These positions were simple propositions. Though well defended they offered no formidable opposition to surprise attacks, save in the case of Rafa.

But with Gaza the case was different. What soul-stirring memories cluster around that ancient town! From time immemorial she has stood on the great warpath of the nations, and was to Africanders the gateway to Asia. What Damascus was in the north, that Gaza has been in the south of Palestine: an *entrepot*, receiving the trade from all routes stretching from Egypt to Arabia.

What conqueror has not seen her? Those mighty Pharaohs, Tothmes and Rameses; Alexander the Great and his ten thousand invincibles; and Pompey with his Roman legions. By this gateway, also, Sennacherib and Nebuchadnezzar entered Egypt. Later on the streets of Gaza echoed the footsteps of Richard Coeur de Lion and his crusaders, in his campaign against Saladin. After him came kings and innumerable nobles from all countries, culminating in the savage onslaughts between the Knights Templars and the Saracens. Last of all, but greatest of all in military genius, came Napoleon in the spring of 1799, on his way to the Euphrates—then back again, making a holocaust of blood and fire to minister at the shrine of his insatiate ambition. Here Samson the Strong performed two of his greatest exploits, and here, too, the great Jewish patriot and hero, whom one has called the William Wallace of Judaism, Judas Maccabeus, fought some of his notable battles against the Syrians.

The defences of modern Gaza justified the confidence of the Turkish and Boche engineers in its impregnability. It was protected by a perfect labyrinth of deeply-cut trenches, with strongly-protected redoubts at frequent intervals, all of which were manned by 10,000 veteran Turks. Heavy batteries were under the control of the Austrians. Every device known to modern warfare was used to defend the position from assault. Large bodies of troops lay within a few miles in readiness to move to its relief if it were in danger. This was the place the Commander-in-Chief of the British forces was asking his men to seize. To take this stronghold needed not only good organisation; speed, dash, the surprise element, daring initiative in the actual conflict—all these were necessary as important factors to success in the undertaking. Even then the day itself must be in sympathy with the attackers to ensure victory.

The great Gaza plain to the south of the Wady Guzzeh presented a panorama of absorbing interest to the spectator as he watched the movements of large bodies of men in the approaching eventide. The sinking sun irradiated the western heavens with indescribable brilliancies, splashing its lovely pigments over an area which reached well up towards the zenith, glorifying even the columnar clouds of dust which trailed skywards from the lines of hurrying troops, who were moving to their positions in readiness for the jump-off at dawn.

Infantry, artillery, supply trains, cavalry, moved across the plains to their predestined places, where they bivouacked in the pale light of a waning crescent moon.

The plan of attack, simply stated, was this. The co-operating forces were under the command of General Dobell. The infantry was to attack at dawn, moving from the canal end of the town, while the cavalry division, under Chauvel, was to make an encircling movement before daybreak—the Australian Light Horse to the right, and the New Zealand Mounteds to the left, were to close the door, so to speak, and prevent the entrance or exit of the enemy. Our interest in this story lying chiefly with the cavalry, we will follow their fortunes.

Two hours before dawn the Anzac cavalry moved from their bivouac in the Wady Guzzeh to carry out the manoeuvre ordered them. The encircling movement had for its objective the cutting off of all enemy communications, and the seizure of certain hills along the coast. In this they were completely successful, occupying positions to the south, east, and north of the Turkish entrenchments. The silence and swiftness of the manoeuvre prevented anything like serious opposition. Before daylight Gaza was invested.

So far all was well; and if only the weather had been favourable to the attackers—or at any rate had remained neutral—there is not much doubt that Gaza, the impregnable, would have been in British hands by nightfall. As it was, however, things turned out otherwise, for with the dawn a thick, impenetrable fog rolled up and covered the plain of Gaza, and greatly retarded the development of the attack. All movements had to be carried out by compass, and it was well after eight before the troops could get going. It was this loss of precious hours at the start which robbed the British of the victory that would assuredly have been theirs had the weather conditions been favourable.

Jack Smith's regiment was in the van of the Light Horse *détour*. Under instructions from his colonel, he gained a position on one of the high hills adjacent to the coast. He had with him half a squadron, and he was to hold it as a post of observation. From this eminence a splendid view was to be had of the whole battle plain. The area on which Gaza stood presented a scene, when the mists had rolled away, of entrancing interest. The town itself, viewed from a distance, revealed none of the squalor which a nearer view presented. Its buildings, though consisting for the most part of evil-smelling hovels, stood glorified in the distant scene. The mosque, with its lofty minarets, was then intact, and rose up a noble specimen of architecture. The gentle slopes upon which the town was built gave character to the picture. Gardens and orchards surrounded the town, enclosed by cactus hedges of monstrous growth. Many of these measured twenty feet in thickness, and were to prove formidable barriers against the assaults of the Light Horsemen.

Looked at from Jack's coign of vantage, the defence—in which these hedges were cleverly utilised—with its system of deep trenches and forward redoubts, appeared to be an impassable barricade. But very soon all sense of the beautiful and the picturesque faded from his mind, and he had eyes only for the infantry, who were now advancing to the main attack. These gallant fellows had several miles to cover before getting within striking distance. Now that the fog had lifted, the advance was in the blazing daylight. The area they had to cross was perfectly level country, offering no protection from the enemy's gunfire. The orchards and fields of ripening barley, which intersected their line of route, were rather a hindrance than a help to them, inasmuch as they served as marks for the enemy's guns. Slowly but surely the gallant infantrymen advanced, despite the heavy losses which resulted from the Turks' concentrated fire.

From his elevated position Jack was, fortunately, able to locate the position of one of the principal batteries. This he signalled to a battery of field guns which the Anzacs had brought with them. In a short time the battery, which was cunningly concealed, began to speak, and before long had silenced the enemy guns thus located.

In the early afternoon an order came to the Australians and New Zealanders, directing them to close in on the enemy. How the men from "down under" obeyed that order will be told in the language of one who was in the thick of the fight:

"...It was with feelings of emotion that we moved out at a gallop, with fixed bayonets, on a charge which carried us almost to the centre of the town, retiring only about eight o'clock in the evening, on word that heavy Turkish reinforcements were within a few miles of the place, and which, had we delayed longer, would have resulted in our being crushed between the two forces. Our first obstacle was the prickly pear. This, with its winding pathways, proved an ideal place for the snipers, as one could be right on top of them without being aware of their whereabouts. Here the bayonet came into use. Crossing a shrapnel-and-rifle-fire area, the attack took the same characteristics —namely, hand-to-hand fighting."

After describing a fine exploit of the New Zealanders in the capture of a Turkish battery after slaughtering the artillerymen, and then turning the captured guns upon the enemy, this eye-witness resumes his account of our advance:

"Just about this time we heard that the Turks were preparing to counter-attack to regain the guns, and our officer on learning this said, 'Righto! We'll attack again and save them the trouble!' When the line was again formed, with the New Zealanders on the left, the order was given to charge. Our objective was a trench hidden behind a large hedge where three roads intersected one another, and opposite to a cemetery. It was grand to see the way the lads got over that space, but the bayonets could not reach through the tangle of the pear. It was simply shoot, muzzle to muzzle.

The dash and vigour was too much for the enemy, who ultimately broke and fled, giving us a chance to hack a pathway through the shrubbery with our bayonets... By this time it was fully 7.30 in the evening, and as the attack on the farthest end of the town had not resulted as desired, the order was given to retire. Although we keenly felt having to leave the town when it was almost won, still, on the whole, as events proved, it was better so. Even in our hurried return we passed within a couple of miles of the relieving force, getting out between the two, with the two guns, you bet, and a large number of prisoners. We just missed capturing their brigadier-general, as he managed to have a little more start. But we caught their colonel and a number of officers. This colonel, I may say, was highly indignant because the chaps that got him made him get out of his carriage and walk, to give the ponies a spell. He afterwards complained to our brigadier of this incident, and said that they actually laughed in his face. Anyhow, he got no change from our old man, who merely told him to take no notice of the lads, as they often told him to go to a warmer climate than Iceland."

CHAPTER XVIII

HOW TIM HOGAN WENT EXPLORING FOR
ST. MICHAELS TOMB

"HELLO, all you dear people! I've just finished reading the batch of letters you sent after receiving my 'wire' to say that the wanderer had returned to the lines in good order and condition.

"In my last letter but one I told you about the Gaza affair. Well, we've been in the thick of it again. I told you in my last letter that things were going to happen shortly. They have happened. All I can say at present is that Gaza still remains in Turkish hands. We found the enemy well prepared for us. He had formed a new system of trenches which played the mischief with us. He got on to us properly and no mistake with the machine-guns. But for all that, we Horsemen gained our objectives. In the long run, however, we had to retire. Had things gone well all round—! But I mustn't say anything about that. Murray gave us Australians and New Zealanders credit for brilliant work. You'll have to guess the rest. The story will be told one of these days. So far as we know our policy for the present will be that of marking time. Gaza is going to be a tough proposition after all. No further advance will be made until adequate reinforcements arrive.

"You must not think for a moment that marking time means doing a loaf. There's no rest for the Light Horse. When our fellows are not doing fatigue work we are on patrol. I dare say you'd like to know something of the character of the country over which we are operating. Our present address is Wady Guzzeh. In one sense it is a long address; for Wady Guzzeh, let me say, is a river. We'd hardly call it by that name in our country. With us it would probably be known as Sandy Creek. Its real meaning is 'The River of Gaza.' It rises away back in the Judean hills, and winds its tortuous way, with as many twists and turns as Tennyson's brook, mainly east, till it meets the sea a few miles south of Gaza. The flow of water is very thin in summer-time, but here and there are decent waterholes with a good deal of vegetation fringing them.

"We are mighty fortunate in holding the river. One cannot help wondering why the Turks abandoned the southern side without a tussle. The beggars had constructed first-class defensive lines, stretching east and west beyond Shellah. Had they stuck to this position we would have been very badly off for water—with the summer, too, in full blast. Thanks, however, to their poor strategy, they abandoned their lines upon our advance from Rafa, and we now control the wady for many miles east. It makes a splendid base for our flank work, to say nothing of its being our principal watering-place.

"To look at there is nothing inviting about the wady—a dry, sandy watercourse, with little vegetation, a pool here and there, contained within precipitous banks. But for all that there's any amount of water underneath the surface. Every unit has its watering-place. For miles along the bed you'll find wired-in areas at frequent intervals, each spot being the recognised water-estate of a particular squadron or regiment. Some of the units are so fearful of their claim being jumped by envious neighbours that they build substantial wire entanglements around them, and padlock the entrance. The value of the wady to us is beyond rubies, and will be better understood when you visualise tens of thousands of horses, camels, and mules along the water area, to say nothing of their riders.

"We have been and are still very busy in elaborating a system of trenches on the north bank of the river. These are designed to run along the slopes, but, of course, I cannot give any particulars. The work has to be done, but none of the men, as far as I know, have developed a fondness for the occupation. It is hardly a subject for poetry, yet one of our fellows has just about hit the nail squarely on the head in describing the ordinary Aussie's feelings about this class of work.

"This is how it begins:
  'When you've eaten dixie stew, and you don't want much to do,
  You are put on fat-i-gue, fat-i-gue, fat-i-gue—
  It's like a day in quod, when the sergeant needs a squad,
     And he hooks you with a nod,
     And you're put on fat-i-gue.'

"Here is the last verse:
  'When the last parade is over, and you're going into clover,
  It's the dickens to discover that it's you for fat-i-gue.
  If I had the beggar now, who invented it, I vow,
     There would be an awful row
     'Bout this blinkin' fat-i-gue.'

"It's not blue ribbon poetry, of course, but, as I said, it puts the thing in a nutshell.

"You must not imagine that the enemy is leaving us in peaceable possession of this place. He sprays us with shrapnel at every opportunity, while his snipers are always on the alert. Many of them are dabs at pinking. This is not a one-sided affair, you may safely bet. We are getting to be adepts at camouflage. Our cunningly-hidden batteries and machine-gun nests keep Jacko's nerves a-jungle.

"On the south side and well under cover are our ambulance and dressing stations, as well as the supply depots. Taken altogether, this is the best camp we Light Horsemen have struck since we started to fight the Turk. Along the northern side of the wady there is a good deal of cultivation. That is to say, there has been. But when the Turks ousted the Arabs and took possession of the river for military purposes, a good deal was destroyed. Still, there are isolated patches of green. Some of the orchards and gardens have been spared. As a result, our menu is occasionally improved by the addition of a melon or a dish of apricots.

"I say, dad, have the papers said anything about the find our fellows made here; or, to speak precisely, at a place called Shellah, on the right bank of the wady, about fourteen miles from Gaza? I may say it is only half a mile from my bivvy, where I am at the present moment.

"Our amateur antiquarians are never tired of telling us that the region of Wady Guzzeh is cram-full of ancient history. Old ruins simply litter the ground. Greek and Roman coins of antiquity can be picked up in places by the bucketful. In a letter I wrote you about a year ago I told you of a find the New Zealanders made at Serapeum, on the bank of the canal, when they exhumed, so to speak, from an ancient and long-buried tomb a portion of the Sacred Bull. All along our trail, from the canal to Rafa, we unearthed from old ruins archaeological curiosities, which will enrich many museums.

"It fell to our Aussie Horsemen the other day to bring to light a hidden treasure, which has made a great stir. While they were engaged in 'fat-i-gue' work, which took the form of digging a trench—or rather extending a Turkish trench— they came upon the remains of an ancient stone building, which experts say is a Greek temple. This temple, it appears, dates back to the sixth century, and was in all probability erected, so the quidnuncs say, during the reign of that famous Emperor of Constantinople, Justinian the Great. The temple is said to be an early Christian church, but the chief interest lies in the uncovering of a very fine mosaic. This I have seen for myself, and without doubt it is a splendid mosaic pavement. The dust of ages had buried it some feet deep; but when this was all removed and the pavement fully exposed and cleaned, its colouring and general preservation were found to be really remarkable.

"Our senior padre, Maitland Woods, the man, you know, who used to have the church at Kangaroo Point, South Brisbane, says it's a splendid specimen of Byzantine art. Worked into the pattern are vases, vines, and several kinds of animals and birds, the whole being surrounded by an ornamental border. The padre says the mosaic is a bit of early Christian symbolism, and is keen on having it lifted and sent to Brisbane. If so you will be able to see it for yourself in the Brisbane Art Gallery.

"By the bye, there's an inscription on the mosaic in Greek characters, the English of which is:

"'This church was constructed during the generation of our great saint, Superior Navios George, the beloved of God, in the year 662.'

"Quite a number hold the saint to have been a local clergyman, but the majority stick out that the inscription stands for the Englishman's patron saint, St. George of the Crusaders, who was born somewhere in Palestine. They hold that this site marks his tomb. It is wonderful what a number of antiquarians have sprung up of late in our division. Everyone who has a bit of leisure is digging at old mounds, which bestrew the place, in search of ancient hidden treasures. And who do you think is the latest victim to the craze? Old Hogan. The last man you'd ever guess. As usual, it's taken a curious twist with him. He's about the best exponent of the serio-comic I've struck. I came across him and one of his cobbers the other day digging at an old ruin which was partly exposed in a mound. I'll put the conversation which was carried on between us, as nearly as I can remember it, in dialogue form.

"'Hello, Tim!' said I; 'what in the name of goodness are you navvying at in this blazing sun?'

"'Faith, Major,' says he, 'we're searchin' for St. Michael's chapel.'

"Laugh! The innocent way in which he said it would have drawn a grin from the sphinx.

"'St. Michael's chapel?' said I, as soon as I could command myself.

"'Yis,' says he. 'Shure, there's nauthin' to laugh at in that.'

"'But, Tim, what makes you think that a chapel's been dedicated hereabouts to St. Michael?'

"'A graate many things, Misther Jack,' he replies. 'Wasn't the English Garge born in Palestine?'

"'So tradition says.'

"'Of course he was. Didn't they find his chapel over here, acrost the way?'

"'A good many believe so.'

"'An' wasn't the Irish St. Michael born over here too?'

"'But, blame it, he wasn't an Irishman, Tim.'

"'He wasn't, wasn't he? Well thin, how did he come be the name?'

"'Blest if I know, old fellow.'

"'Well thin, I'll inform ye. He was an Irish Jew. Did ye niver hear tell of wan?'

"'Yes, you grinning ape; you're one yourself. But that doesn't help your story much.'

"'Excuse me, Major, but I'll have to tache ye a little ancient histhry. When I was a spalpeen livin' at Curribumby, New South Wales, where I was brought up be me payrunts, I heard Father O'Grady at Mass wan Sunday givin' his histhry—I mane Michael's. He said he lived way back in Daniel the prophet's time, an' fought for him against the Persians. Later on, the praste says, he fought the Dhragon. It's gospel thrue, Major, for I mind he read a full account of the fight in Revelations. An' all this was long before Garge's day, his riv'rince said; for the Englishman came centuries afther. Now, if that's thrue, an' it's in the Howly Book, moind ye, doesn't that put Garge's nose out of jint?'

"'You make out a strong case, Dan O'Connell,' I said, when I could speak. Several fellows, drawn by the sound of our yapping, stood round, and chivvied Tim. Hogan has a wide reputation, I can tell you.

"'Still, Tim,' continued I, 'you haven't proved what you asserted at the beginning, you know.'

"'Well, if I haven't, faith I'll prove it this very minute.'

"'Prove what?'

"'Prove that St. Michael comes before St. Gorge; also that they're always found together.'

"'Get off the scratch, then, quick and lively.'

"'Tell me, Major, phwat does G.C.M.G. stand for—the letthers the owld gin'ral has tacked to his name?'

"'That's easy, Tim. Grand Commander of St. Michael and St. George. It's the title of his knighthood.'

"'Thrue for ye, sir. Now tell me who it was that gave him the letthers.'

"'Why, the King, of course.'

"'Which name thin, sir, stands first?'

"'Why, St. Mich—you old rascal!'

"'Is the King right or wrong? Come now, Major dear?'

"'You have me at a dead end, Tim. I throw up the sponge. The King can do no wrong.'

"'An' so, Major an' byes, that's why I'm explorin' for St. Michael's chapel. Both are credited wid killin' the Dhragon. Both were born in Palestine. Their names come close together like twin brothers, in a sinse. Wherever one is, ye'll find the other. That's why I'm rootin' here for Michael's tomb widin sight of Garge's.'

"At that, dad, I had to retire as gracefully as I could from the scene, leaving Tim with the full honours of war.

"LATER.

"What do you think? Our old Chief is to be relieved, and General Allenby is succeeding him. He comes hot from the West Front, where he gained a great name, so it's said. We hear he's a tremendous hustler, with a genius for organisation. He's one of Kitchener's men, the same as Murray. That in itself is a guarantee of efficiency. My fountain pen has run dry. Love to all.

—Your
JACK."

CHAPTER XIX

HOW JACK LED HIS MERRY MEN ON A RECONNAISSANCE

"ARE you in, Jock?"

"Hello there!"

Throwing aside the door-flap, Jack Smith entered Mackenzie's bivvy in the late afternoon, and found his chum busily engaged in letter-writing.

"Writing love-letters, eh?"

"Don't be so jolly inquisitive, Smithie. To what am I indebted for the honour of a visit from my major? Thought you'd gone over to Headquarters."

"So I had. I've just come from there in company with the colonel. Chauvel's got a job for us."

"For *us*?"

"Yes, my captain, for us. That is to say, I'm to make a reconnaissance with a troop, and am giving you the chance to come in."

"Thanks awfully, old man. Ready for anything, from pitch-an'-toss to manslaughter. When do we start?"

"About an hour after sunset. Get B troop together, old fellow. It means two days' rations. See that the neddies get a double ration at their supper. And oh, I say! Don't forget to detail a couple of stretcher-bearers. Ring in Hogan for one if he's available."

"All serene. They'll be ready. Where are you off to in such a violent hurry?" For Jack had hardly given his orders ere he was disappearing through the doorway.

"Over to see the colonel. He has some plans I want to see."

It might be thought that with the increase of British aeroplanes all reconnaissances would now be made from the air. Without reflecting in any degree upon the value of the aeroplane as the eyes of the forces, there were enemy secrets that could only be penetrated by the movements of a well-ordered patrol. Such was that which was now on the eve of going forth under the command of Jack Smith.

Jack's work of a similar nature in the Maghara Hills, and later between Romani and El Arish, had brought him into great favour with the divisional Headquarters, and he was often entrusted with stunts which called for unusual qualities.

In the present instance he was to take a small mobile patrol wide out on the right flank, and if practicable make a circuit of Beersheba. There were cunningly devised redoubts and outposts, upon the exact location and strength of which the Headquarters Staff had no reliable information, despite the good work of the airmen. To ensure success in the contemplated movement it was necessary to discover the well-laid traps provided by the Boches and Turks.

The influence of the German and Austrian officers, who had by this time leavened the Turkish forces, had created a thoroughness and skill in the system of defence, General Allenby, therefore, was leaving nothing to chance. The right flank, it is true, had been well patrolled within limits for many weeks. The one now ordered was an extra, and intended to cover ground hitherto untouched. The plans to which Jack had referred in his brief conversation with Jock Mackenzie in the latter's bivvy, were those supplied by the airmen. There were places in the aerial photographs marked "suspicious." To these as well as to other things Jack was to direct his attention.

The small column of thirty picked men started out along the dry bed of Wady Guzzeh, proceeding in an easterly direction before venturing to cross over to the north bank. The British were being well watched by a determined foe. In addition to a large squadron of aeroplanes of the newest types, Turkish cavalry spread themselves over the country, using the local Bedouins to assist them in their spying purposes. There were several regiments in and around Beersheba composed of infantry and cavalry. Their mobile squadrons covered a wide radius.

To know this is to appreciate the nature of the work entrusted to the youthful major and his men. Consistently with caution, speed was essential to success. Despite every care and the astuteness with which the leader was gifted, and those rare instincts which he possessed to a remarkable degree, the unexpected was still possible. A crisis might happen which would upset all plans, and when naught but headlong recklessness would avail.

The delicate nature of the patrol, together with the hardships and perils to be faced in carrying out his mission, were not hidden from the leader. Yet there was no brooding anxiety or depression of spirits to be seen in his bearing as he rode at the head of his tiny column along the river bed, and later on, over the arid and waterless desert.

As for the troopers, it was enough for them that Major Smith was in command. This was not the first affair by many that they had carried out under his leadership. They had perfect faith in him. Let happen what might, it would come out all right. Trust him for discovering a firm road over any bog of difficulty or danger they might encounter.

The "walers," as the horses bred on the great Australian plains are called, have proved themselves to be the very finest type for cavalry purposes. They contain strains of the best blood of the English racing type. Under climatic and other conditions they have developed into a distinct type of horse which for intelligence, speed, and endurance is unequalled for war purposes.

Every Light Horseman, either to the manner born or by years of experience, is an accomplished rider. His love for his steed does not come second even to that of the Arab. Between man and horse there grows a kindred feeling which produces a perfect understanding. Both man and horse express the qualifes of their early environment.

The fabled centaurs did not present a more complete co-ordination of man and beast than the Aussie and his waler.

From this it will be readily seen that what Jack's patrol lacked in numerical strength it made up in efficiency. Indeed, its smallness was altogether in its favour for secret movement, while, at the same time, it was capable of striking hard blows at larger bodies of troops, should necessity compel.

The route taken by Major Jack was one with which he was familiar. After leaving the wady he swung to the north-east for some miles and then turned in an easterly direction. The brilliant starlight afforded sufficient light for swift advance. Each man was inured to desert warfare by never-to-be-forgotten experiences in the Sinai Peninsula. Consequently the tiny force moved in strict silence and with wonderful celerity. No horse stumbled or neighed, no metal clinked, no voice rose above a murmur. The advance more nearly resembled a company of ghouls on phantom steeds than flesh-and-blood men mounted on real horses.

The course taken avoided certain outposts that were well known to the British. Calling Mackenzie to his side, the leader engaged him in a conversation on matters relating to the reconnaissance. While it was comparatively easy to avoid known places, there was no providing against the unknown dangers which they might encounter at any moment. Roving Bedouins in the pay of the enemy, and secret occupations by the Turks, were two of the linking dangers which were possible contingencies. Needless to say, every eye and ear of the column now travelling in loose formation—yet not straggling—was alert to detect any approaching peril.

Jack suddenly ceased his murmured conversation with his fellow-officer, and pulled rein while he gave a low, sharp command—"Halt!"

The word ran along the moving unit in a subdued ripple of sound. The troop came to a dead stop. Not a word was spoken, nor a sound made save the faint creaking of the saddles as they yielded to the breathing of the horses.

"What is it, Jack?" whispered Mackenzie to his leader.

"Camels."

"Where? Can you see 'em?"

"No need to see 'em. Smell 'em."

"By George, yes."

The pungent malodour assailed all nostrils. The men needed no further evidence of the cause of the sudden stoppage of their advance. They were in the vicinity of camels. Of these there was no other sign than the one stated. Officers and men stood to attention and both eyes and ears were strained to their limits in the attempt to locate the animals. Were they in the vicinity of a Bedouin camp; or was it a bivouac of Turkish camelry? They could detect no sound of moving beasts. The only thing to indicate their presence was the acrid smell borne upon the night wind. The breeze was faint and fitful, but there was sufficient to mark the direction.

Jack's first impulse was to ride forward and investigate for himself. He quickly checked that, however. He must remain with his men. He whispered an order to his companion:

"Dismount Yellow Billy and Thargomindah Frank, and send them along to me."

Mackenzie quickly executed the order, and in a few seconds the men indicated stood before their major at salute.

Leaning over his saddle, Jack addressed them in low tones:

"I want you fellows to do a bit of scouting. You, Frank, move out to the left across yonder ridge. You, Billy, work ahead a bit, and then, if you see nothing, work round and towards Frank, who in the same event will edge round towards you. Take off your spurs, as there's a lot of brush on the slope of the ridge. There's a donga on the other side. Search it well."

Quickly removing their spurs, they handed them to Mackenzie and moved cautiously forward in absolute silence. Before many moments their indistinct forms had faded into invisibility. They knew their business. Yellow

Billy was a half-caste, who, previous to enlisting, had been employed as a tracker in the Queensland Mounted Police, while Thargomindah Frank was born and bred in the cattle country of the Far West, where he had obtained celebrity as a bushman, expert in all the devices of his craft.

Jack knew his men, not only by name. He had a genius for summing up a man's character and capabilities. Without being in any sense a Paul Pry, he got to know his men as few officers are able. This knowledge was of the greatest service to him. On the present occasion, although there was hardly a man in the troop who would not have done good work had he been called upon, he was able to select at a moment's notice two outstanding troopers for this particular job.

"Say, Jack, how'd you know about the donga?" said Mackenzie in muffled tones, as the men passed out of sight on their errand.

"That's easy. For the past half-hour I've been following the track along which M'Thirst and I were carried by the Bedouins when they pinched us."

"My goodness! You don't mean to tell me that you recognised the track in the dark?"

"Oh, there's nothing much in that. 'Member the hill we passed on the left, back a piece?"

"Yes."

"And the creek with the pebbly bottom, that had a single tree growing right in the centre of the bed?"

"Yes. I remarked on it."

"Well, those were two of the spots out of many that I recognised as we passed along. This ridge, too. It is quite familiar to me. I can see the deep donga which lies on the other side as clearly in my mind as if I were actually looking at it. The track passes the lip of the crater-like formation."

"Suppose a detachment is located there. What do you propose to do?"

"It all depends on the report the fellows bring. I'm not going to fight if it can possibly be avoided."

It did not take the spies long to achieve their object. They quickly located the supposed enemy. Each made his observation independently of the other. Within a quarter of an hour they returned with the information required. During these operations they had not sighted one another.

Their reports agreed substantially. A party of Turkish camelry occupied the spot, and, judging from the appearance of the camp, it was the rendezvous of a patrol. They reckoned the strength to be about one hundred and fifty, including a machine-gun section. Yellow Billy had detected the latter from his vantage-ground. Furthermore, sentries were posted to guard against surprise.

Jack's mind was quickly made up. To attack would be a rash undertaking; for, even if they were successful, they would in all probability pay dearly. Besides, they would be encumbered with prisoners and wounded. And at the same time their object would probably be defeated. No, they were not out to fight. Though it went against the grain to leave this nest behind him, it was the only thing to do.

But to pass along the trail would be a hazardous undertaking. Even were they to slip by unseen and unheard, their tracks at dawn would betray them. These patrolling Turks were not to be taken lightly. They knew all the points of the game. The troop's tracks would be interpreted as those of an enemy, and in less than no time they would be hot-foot on the trail. The thought of such an eventuality was anything but agreeable to Jack, nor did he intend to offer any such chances.

In obedience to the order quietly given, the men faced about and retreated some distance before making a wide *détour*, by which they avoided the enemy. The plateau across which they rode was intersected with dry gullies. They followed one of these for some distance and then left it, pursuing an angle which brought them to their original line of march, a couple of miles ahead of the donga.

By this time the night was paling in indication of the approaching dawn. According to Jack's estimate they had advanced to the south-east of Beersheba. So far the adventure had been all that could be wished for. They had advanced through the night with only one check. They had located one post hitherto unknown to them. They had so far managed to avoid detection, and had already covered a considerable portion of the ground mapped out for them. True, they had had the advantage of the darkness, and would soon have to take all the risks of passing through enemy territory in broad daylight. On the other hand, daylight had its good points. Given ordinary luck, the leader was sanguine of accomplishing his errand.

CHAPTER XX

HOW THE PARTY FOUND WATER, AND HOW THEY ESCAPED A TURKISH COLUMN

HALTING at the base of a high hill, the troop dismounted. Their first act was to sling the nosebags round their horses' heads. After this duty had been performed they broke into their tucker bags.

Leaving the men under the charge of Mackenzie, and taking Yellow Billy with him, Jack utilised the short break by climbing the hillside, which rose steeply to some five hundred feet. It did not take him long to reach the summit, which was bare of vegetation. The sun was already crimsoning the east and the pale light of the dawn was momentarily growing stronger. Objects could now be seen within a radius of a couple of miles. As the light mists covering the depressions lifted or thinned out to invisibility the hidden portions stood further revealed.

The keen watcher was mostly interested in the country lying to the north and north-east. As the range of visibility extended, making clear a wider area, he keenly scrutinised each portion. As far as could be seen there was no sign of occupation in the vicinity of the hill. The country hereabouts was sterile, consequently—except for wandering bands of Bedouins or passing Turkish soldiers —there was little or no danger to be apprehended from settlements.

Having satisfied himself of their immediate safety, he bent his gaze upon the more distant scene. Here he was instantly rewarded. Miles away he discerned the movement of minute figures. Almost at the same moment Billy called his attention to these Lilliputian objects. Although for general purposes he preferred to trust to his natural eyesight, he did not disdain glasses when particular concentration was required. Unslinging his glasses and focusing them upon the tiny moving atoms, the result confirmed his opinion. It was a Turkish patrol moving in towards Beersheba. He sensed it to be a night-patrol, which had probably confined itself to a limited area over which any attempted British raid would be likely to pass under cover of the night.

They were able to detect three or four places of occupation in the rapidly increasing radius. Before long Beersheba itself became visible. It looked at first a mere grey, nebulous patch, hardly distinguishable from the surrounding terrain. Soon, however, it began to resolve itself into a cluster of buildings. In addition were rows of military tents and other buildings for the soldiers. Beyond these were the enclosing strong lines of defence. Without doubt Beersheba was a difficult nut to crack.

While to all appearance the country to the north was clear of outlying forces, Jack was perfectly aware that not much reliance could be placed upon this outward seeming. There was a lot of broken country which might easily hold troops, and in all probability did, who could not be seen from the present coign of vantage. The investigation must proceed from the general to the particular. Without being told in so many words by his chief, he drew the conclusion that his present work was preliminary to a big raid, the success of which would depend to a great extent upon an accurate knowledge of the obstacles that would have to be faced.

Having thoroughly scanned the area stretching north over the plateau, and north-east to the broken country, Jack mapped out in his mind the course of their route-march. He had debated in his mind the question of lying *perdu* through the day, and travelling only at night, but dismissed it for these reasons. First, the country from now on was unfamiliar to him, and, though he had access to military maps, too much reliance could not be placed upon them. They were more or less imperfect. Daylight travel, under these conditions, would be safer than night travel. Then again, they might easily pass danger-spots in the dark without being aware of them. His orders were to locate all the positions held by the enemy within the area over which the British troops would operate.

For these reasons, save for short, necessary halts, it was his intention to travel without intermission. He would use every second of daylight to cover as much ground as possible, making his longest stops in the night.

Just before descending, Billy drew his attention to a tiny object about a mile due east.

"Looks like a well-head, Major."

"You're right, Billy. It's a well-head sure enough. It'll be a godsend if it's not a dry one. It'll be a big throw-in for the horses."

Descending rapidly, the pair rejoined their companions, and without any delay moved forward on a route which, in a few moments, brought them to the well.

The wells, for there were two, were a little to the east of an inviting valley, with a high, rocky ridge on the north side. The valley had patches of green sward most refreshing to the eyes. The little, fertile patches stood out in beautiful relief to the sterile surroundings which otherwise marked the locality.

The wells were unequal in size, the smaller being stoned, and measuring about six feet in diameter. If was fully twenty feet deep, and contained about eight feet of water. The larger well was more ancient. Many of the huge slabs of stone which formed its walls had broken away and fallen to the bottom. The stone on the unbroken side was deeply scored with parallel marks. These flutings, if they may be so described, were a couple of inches deep, being made by the friction of the rope in lowering and raising buckets. They bore eloquent though silent testimony to the great antiquity of the well. How many hundreds of ropes had worn to breaking point during the process of the centuries? What an innumerable succession of flocks and herds had watered here—flocks and herds owned by the godly Abraham, Isaac, and Jacob, to go back no farther!

Several stone troughs stood about, some of which were broken cisterns which could hold no water. A few, however, were in an excellent condition. In a short time the horses were drinking to their hearts' content of the cool, sweet water. The men, too, made the most of their opportunity. When they had slaked their thirst they refilled their water-bags, for who could say whether another such opportunity would occur?

Surrounding the wells were several stone walls more or less broken down, justifying the adage that "everything goes to ruin in an Arab's hands." In addition were cairns, evidently old storehouses for grain, and stables for animals. These, together with the ruins of stone houses, betokened a one-time settlement.

Kicking carelessly at a small mound of broken pottery a short distance from the well, Jock Mackenzie uncovered a snake. Now snakes are numerous in Palestine, most of them, fortunately, being non-venomous. Still, a stranger were wise not to speculate on the character of a serpent when meeting one in the Holy Land. Either give him the whole countryside to roam over, if he feel so inclined, or despatch him with a well-placed blow. The one in question was killed without any scruple. Although the men had met with many varieties, including cobras and the horned viper, this was an entirely new specimen to them. It was about a yard long and was covered with fiery-looking spots.

"Say, Jack," remarked Mackenzie to his chum, "this is a bit of a curiosity. Look at the crimson spots on its skin. Wish I'd a bottle. I'd take him along to Charlie Barrett, who knows every bird and reptile in creation."

"Be jabers, Captain," said Tim Hogan, who had joined a group of gazers, "shure, there's no need to consult anywan about the class of this animal. Faith, but 'tis worse nor a tiger-snake or a death-adder."

"Good heavens, Tim! When did you qualify for an ornithologist?"

"Indade, thin, you might call me a worse name nor that, sir."

"But, Tim, how d'ye know whether it's poisonous or non-poisonous?"

"I'll till ye thin, Captain dear. I was radin' about the Israelites in the Bible in the Y.M.C.A. hut wan day. Ye'll remimber whin they mutinied aginst God an' Moses in the wilderness, an' started a sthrike aginst their tucker? Well thin, didn't the Almighty punish thim by sendin' 'fiery sepents' among them? They bit the sthrikers right an' lift, so they did, till thousands of thim died. There 'tis in the Owld Book, in the histhry of the Israelites as they wandered hereabouts. An' if ye don't believe me—!"

"Carry on!"

The major's imperative cut short the disquisition upon the snake question. Mounting their steeds, they were soon threading their way along the tortuous valley which was formed by the long, sloping banks of a dry watercourse. In the rainy season this wady became a raging torrent. As they passed along they observed at intervals the remains of what were at one time heavy stone walls. These were built across the wady at regular intervals to arrest the rush of water, which could then be used in irrigating the fertile levels. It pointed to a time anterior to Arab occupation.

The column moved cautiously yet swiftly forward. There was nothing haphazard about their advance. Jack's brain, for the present, held only a mental map of their route. He was travelling north, well to the east of Beersheha, yet not too far to miss any position of a formidable nature. He took advantage of every hill to scan the country ahead. By this, without actually altering the direction of the march, he was able to modify it to the benefit of the course.

It was not until the early afternoon that he received the first check. He had halted the troop at the base of a hill which rose much higher than the surrounding hillocks. Ascending this in company with Mackenzie to make some observations, he was astonished to see, rapidly approaching, a troop of Turkish cavalry. The direction taken by these men would bring them, within a few minutes, face to face with the Light Horse.

Had it been an ordinary occasion he would have rejoiced at the sight. All the profit of surprise would have been with him. The Turks would have fallen into a trap. The men, too, would have wished for nothing better than the chance of overriding an equal number of the enemy. That, however, was not to be entertained for a moment. Up to the present the reconnaissance had been a success. He was now well abreast of Beersheba, which lay under his eyes less than five miles to the west. To throw away his chances of completing the big order given him by the general, under any pretence but that of absolute necessity, were an act of inexcusable folly. Flight, and only flight, would save the situation.

The two youths almost jumped from the crest to the base of the hill in a stride. In less than a minute from the time the enemy was sighted, the Aussies were rattling round the base of the hill at right angles to the line of the enemy's advance. Fortunately for them, the country for some miles round was thickly covered with stunted vegetation. No one but those accustomed to sign-reading would discover their tracks; but the Turks composing the cavalry units were not gifted in that direction. Farther back, where they had travelled along a well-defined road for some distance, the greatest novice that rode could not help seeing horse-tracks in the soft dust. Even then the chances were that the observers would not connect the revealing hoof-marks with a hostile band. They would be regarded as the tracks of one of their own units.

The moment he halted the troop, he despatched Captain Mackenzie and Thargomindah Frank to the hilltop to watch the Jackoes' movements. It became evident, however, that these fellows had no suspicion of the proximity of a hostile band. The watchers remained until the Turks had advanced a couple of miles upon their way before returning to the unit with their report.

It had been Jack's intention to halt for a brief rest at the first safe place. This he now gave effect to. The spot was well off the ordinary track, and was surrounded by steep ridges. It was one of those bowl-like depressions often to be met with in broken country. The enemy might ride within fifty yards of them and have no suspicion of their presence.

His plan was to lie *perdu* until after dark. The critical part of their adventure was now to be played. They were to edge in on Beersheba as closely as they dared. To attempt this in the daylight would be mad stupidity. Already, as the present close shave indicated, he was taking undue risks. His momentary glimpse of Beersheba from the hilltop brought home to him the imminence of the dangers which now confronted him. Henceforward his advance must be as silent, yet as sure, as the flight of a nighthawk.

Meanwhile, the rest would be of the utmost service to both horse and man. The heat had exacted its toll from the travellers. They had been, with scarcely any intermission, some twenty hours in the saddle. Though their advance was not at any time forced, it had been attended with a mental strain. Consequently there came a moment when even these hardy, weatherproof, light-hearted men became conscious of a certain tension to which both body and mind contributed. Though not nearly at the limit of their endurance, their strained features gave an outward and visible sign. As for the beasts, the reek of the sweaty leather bore abundant witness.

CHAPTER XXI

HOW THE SPIES PROGRESSED, AND HOW JACK RECONNOITRED THE REDOUBT

THE troopers would have liked to relieve their horses by removing the saddles and packs. That, however, was not to be thought of. To off-saddle in the enemy's territory, with the possibility of attack at any moment, would be inviting disaster. The walers, perforce, had to be content with the nosebag and rest. The men were better placed in that their water-bags contained some stock of the precious fluid.

When their steeds had been attended to, and hunger and thirst appeased, they threw themselves upon the ground, and slept as only such veterans can. The only ones who did not join in the seductive occupation were the sentries, who were posted at intervals around the donga, and Smith and Mackenzie. The latter, when all the dispositions of the temporary camp were made, reascended the hill together.

The patrol had now reached a critical stage. While the Turkish defences to the west and south of Beersheba were fairly well known, there was a scarcity of information regarding the position eastward and northward. They had reached a spot about the stronghold on its eastern side, and it was now incumbent upon the leader to gain accurate information of the eastern defences. To enable him to determine his immediate course, he decided to make a careful inspection from the hilltop while the light remained good.

After the youths had gained a place, where, without being seen by an enemy eye, they could get an uninterrupted view of the prospect, they settled down to a methodical scrutiny of Beersheba and its environs. There were few objects of any magnitude which escaped the clear sight of these bushmen, so much of whose life had been lived in open spaces, and whose senses had been quickened by their calling of kangaroo hunters. In the present instance their concentrated examination was not without good fruit. Both men had glasses, but, save to confirm some conclusion, Jack rarely used them. He could trust his eyes to sight any object within a possible range. Beersheba was about five miles distant, though it seemed much nearer owing to their lofty view-point. The buildings stood out distinctly.

In addition to the scattered vestiges of ancient buildings, and the broken walls, were the modern buildings erected by the Turks shortly before the war. They quickly picked out the Serai or Government House, and the post and telegraph houses. But they were much more concerned to observe the fortifications made by the Jackoes since the outbreak of the war. The strategic importance of the place quickly came home to them when they realised it as the place of junction of the main road through central Palestine, with the railway traversing the maritime plain. The town they now viewed was not on the original site. The Beersheba of the Patriarchs was some distance to the east. It is a hill, known as Tell-es-Saba. This was now an outpost strongly fortified by the Germans.

Although bent on a stern military errand, the sight of this historic spot brought feelings in the minds of the youths which stirred them to an emotion of veneration. The first books of the Old Testament had been diligently read by numbers of men whose keenness was kindled by trending on the historic soil and passing along the ancient ways. From the start of his work in Palestine, Jack had sought to make himself acquainted with Biblical literature bearing upon the places of antiquity. Here, for some moments as he lay with fixed gaze upon the two sites, there came before him and his chum visions of the great actors in the early dramas of the human race. Abraham, Isaac, Jacob, and later on Samuel and Elijah had been sojourners by the wells of Beersheba. Sentiment, however, must not be allowed to overlay duty. The present task was to find out all that was possible about Beersheba and its defences.

The lads noted the activity at the railhead, and were able to form some estimate of the strength of the forces in the encampment. Among other things, they made out a clump of eucalyptus trees—the only trees, as a matter of fact, to be found in the otherwise treeless neighbourhood. Jock vowed he smelt the pungent odour of the gums.

When they had minutely scanned the defences immediately surrounding the base, they gave their attention to the country outlying. It was not long before Jack detected what appeared to be a strong outpost lying between a couple of parallel ridges. It was fully seven miles from the hilltop in a north-easterly direction. It was patent that great pains had been taken to conceal it as much as possible. He had no recollection of seeing it marked on any plan.

Here, then, before them lay an immediate duty—that of determining the strength of this new position.

"We've got our work cut out for us, old man," exclaimed Jock, when they had spent some time in endeavouring to determine the features of the post. "Nothing but a near view will give us what we want to know."

"You're right, sonny."

"What do you propose to do then?"

"Ride up to the lip and have a good look," said Jack laughingly.

"Cut that out," replied Jock testily. "You've got a plan, you old beggar. Out with it."

"What I've said in fun I mean in earnest. We cannot leave this post without ascertaining its strength: not only man-strength, but gun-strength. You may bet your last coin that they've masked any batteries they have placed there. It means, old man, that we make a close investigation."

"Meaning?"

"As soon as the darkness sets in we'll start, and keep going until we reach those ridges yonder, where we'll camp. It'll bring us abreast the post, and ought to be a good place for halting the men. Once there, I'll leave you in charge and do a hit of spying."

"But, I say, Jack, you don't mean to say that you're going to leave the troop, and do the job upon your lonesome? Why, there's a dozen of us who could—"

"Jock Mackenzie, the greatest compliment you ever paid me was when you told the brigadier the other day that you'd back me for scouting against the whole division."

"And stick to it. But for all that, you're in command. Is it right for you to take this risk when another could do it effectively, if not quite as well as yourself?"

"I quite understand you, old man. Don't think for one moment that I'm inclined to depreciate the ability of the rest of you. There are a score of men who could do it equally well, and some of them much better, without doubt. I suppose, though, you're wondering how I can justify myself to the chief should anything go wrong while I'm away. I've thought of that myself. Still, for all that, I feel that I ought to run the hazard. I'm a fellow, you know, of strong instincts. My instinct is telling me at the present moment to take it on. It has rarely deceived me, and I'm in a mood to yield to it. This is a matter of great importance, and I'll take the risk."

Nothing more was said. Jock knew from experience that when his pal made up his mind to a certain course a bullock team could not move him.

It wanted an hour to sunset when they rejoined the unit. In two hours or so they would he on the move. After changing the sentries, Jack threw himself on the softest part of the ground available to snatch an hour's sleep. He was dividing watches with Jock. In a moment he was dead to the world. Blotted out from his mind were all the questions and the problems of his adventure, and he enjoyed a full hour of log-like repose for both mind and body. It needed not the call of his man to awaken him at the time appointed. He had the precious gift of sleeping when he willed, and waking when he willed to wake. The moment he awoke all his faculties were alert. When his major arose Jock Mackenzie tumbled to mother earth in imitation of his chief.

The spy-column had been moving through the dark for some hours. The sky, which was brilliantly studded with innumerable stars, was being now dimmed with a haze which betokened a change in the weather. Drifting clouds soon appeared and covered large areas of the overhead expanse. This change was as welcome as it was unexpected. While it slowed their rate of progress, and hid possible danger-points from them, it was friendly in that it shortened the range of visibility. This, of course, would weigh in Jack's favour when he set out on his hazardous task.

The force by this time was nearing the spot selected for the halt. Two short ridges meeting in a curve, with the convex side facing the Turkish redoubt, made an admirable place for concealment in the dark. This brought the troops within a mile of the objective.

Halting his men as they neared the locality, Jack sent out Yellow Billy and Thargomindah Frank in charge of Sergeant Coombes, an old Boer War veteran. The object was to search the pocket behind the boomerang-shaped ridge. Now that he was on the eve of a critical advance it behoved him to leave nothing to chance. Luck at the best was a fickle friend, apt to desert one in the hour of his greatest need.

The men soon returned with an "all clear" report, and the small force occupied the sheltered position formed by the curving ridges. That done, Jack immediately posted men on the ridge, with a small vedette well out to the rear.

Having made his dispositions, Jack was prepared for instant departure. The men were not ignorant of the nature of his undertaking. Not one of them but would have been proud to accompany him. Still, if he were bent on acting by himself—well, good luck to him. Their confidence in his ability relieved them of all fear for him.

It was arranged that Jock should station himself on the tiny plateau where the ridges converged. This gave him the advantage of being in touch with the sentries on the ridge, as well as the troops in the hollow below. Jack had further arranged with his captain to signal him by torch-flash, should necessity compel it.

Jock watched his companion melt into the darkness, as he advanced noiselessly on foot down the ridge in the direction of the outpost, with some compunction. Yet there was no element of misgiving or foreboding in his feelings. No one knew better than he the coolness, intrepidity, and resourcefulness of his mate. Mackenzie himself was not lacking in these qualities. The very possession of them made him the more appreciative of the shining qualities of the other. The compunction had regard to the head of the column leaving his command for any such object. Jack himself would find no justification for it save on the ground of necessity. Had the necessity arisen?

On leaving his men, Jack made his way with due caution and with little difficulty until he reached a point within a short distance of his objective. The difficulties became apparent when he entered upon the practical part of his work. The whole area of the heavens was now cloud-covered, and the darkness cut two ways. While it tended to his invisibility, it shrouded at the same time the objects which he wished to locate.

What he had principally to determine was the character of the post. Was it armed for defensive purposes, or was it simply an observation post, serving at the same time as a centre of patrol work? If the former, there would be artillery. To find out, he must get within. Here, then, was the nature of his work: its perilous character. How was he to gain entrance? That would depend on circumstances. He was wedded to no plan. He would be guided by what he found. He was now near enough to hear the sound of voices. These were intermittent, rising and falling almost in measured cadence. Above this, however, there were outbursts of laughter and singing. These noises reassured him. They were an intimation that no suspicion was held. No one, so far, had sighted him and given the alarm.

Proceeding with the utmost caution, he now advanced to an area of wire entanglements which enclosed a strong redoubt. His immediate task was to get through the maze. This, under the most advantageous circumstances, could not be carried out without noise. Noise would attract the notice of the guard. What chance, then, would he have of carrying out his object?

But none of these things unduly moved Jack. One thing at a time. First of all he must search for an opening. The chances were that one existed. It didn't appear that the Turks were apprehensive of any danger. He was now coasting the outer edge of the entanglement, and cautiously feeling for signs of an opening, when he suddenly stood rigid and motionless, eyes and ears alert.

Someone was approaching!

Of this there was as yet no outward manifestation, either by sight or sound, but for all that he knew, more by instinct or intuition than by any definable sense. He seemed to feel the presence of somebody, and his nose presently confirmed this belief. There came to his nostrils an indefinable yet easily recognisable odour of the body. It was a brand that was common to the Eastern, and took on an overproof quality in the desert Bedouin.

To be forewarned was to be forearmed. Revolver in hand, he awaited the approach of the unknown. Was there one individual only, or were there numbers? He had no chance of determining this. Whoever the person might be, he was in all probability friendly to the Turks. He could hardly think of a Bedouin who was hostile to them prowling about in such close proximity to them; or even a band of them. Besides, the Bedouins of the neighbourhood would be sure to be in the pay of the Turks.

Yet, argue as he would in his mind while he stood thus as silent as the moon, he felt absolutely certain that one of these fellows was within a few yards of him. More than that, the chap was fringing the wires. Placing his hand lightly upon the entanglements, he became conscious of a vibration, caused by the contact of some moving object. Whoever it was, was engaged in the same game as himself —fishing for an opening.

While he thus stood, a form emerged from the darkness within an arm's length. The stranger sighted his opponent too late. A pistol-point was pressed firmly against his body over his heart, while a low, menacing voice hissed in Arabic:

"Hands up!"

CHAPTER XXII

HOW JACK FOUND EID, AND HOW BEERSHEBA WAS WON

UPON his watch-tower, just as the night showed the first glimmer of dawn, his face set steadfastly towards Beersheba, his eyes aching with the strain of his earnest gaze through the livelong night, stood Jock Mackenzie. Close by was Yellow Billy, whom he had called to his side during the night. Though not unduly anxious, yet as the hours sped and dawn approached with no signal from his mate, certain misgivings arose in his mind. Had all gone well? Had Jack been outwitted? It is only fair to say that, though thus assailed, the youth did not surrender his judgment to any such suggestions of his imagination. Nevertheless, he was greatly relieved when a single, momentary flash shot through the vanishing dark, indicating the return of the spy.

"There's two of 'em, Captain," exclaimed Yellow Billy in low tones a few minutes later, when two indistinct figures made a blotch on the dull grey of the early dawn.

"There are two, as you say. The major is one for certain, for that was his signal agreed upon. Now who on earth can be with him? Some lurking Turk he's bagged, I'll wager a penny."

Mackenzie made a bad guess. It was the half-caste who first identified Jack's companion.

"By gum!" almost shouted he, as the indistinct forms took definite shape. "Blest if the second bloke ain't the old nigger, Eid!"

Eid it was beyond a doubt. Jack, however, did not volunteer any information. As soon as he reached speaking distance he gave a sharp command: "Call in the sentries and get the men on the move in double quick time." Explanations could wait over.

This was a command, and not knowing what lay behind it, Jock turned on the salute and gave immediate effect to the order. He was, however, considerably surprised when his leader, addressing the men—who were standing to—on his arrival, told all and sundry in a few words that the object of the patrol had been achieved, and that they would start at once upon the backward track. Just at this moment half a dozen Bedouins appeared, mounted on camels. They proved to be Eid's men, one of whom was leading the sheikh's beast.

When the column had got well on its way, Jack related to his companion the happenings of the night. Eid, he said, knew him the moment he spoke. The major's pleasure was undisguised when the supposed enemy turned out to be his close and tried friend. His delight was heightened a few minutes later when, on reaching a safe place, Eid, in a few words, put him in possession of certain facts.

It will be remembered that the Bedouin remained behind when Jack and M'Thirst took their departure in the aeroplane. He proceeded at once to put his intentions into practice. It was not long before he was in possession of his camel; and then, proceeding by devious paths, he fixed upon the member of Yacob's band who had "broken salt" by a traitorous act. The punishment was condign and in accordance with desert laws.

Having thus achieved his objects, the old man leisurely worked his way through the Turkish lines, sometimes alone, and at others in the company of nomads friendly to the Turks. In this way he amassed a considerable amount of information. For the preceding three days he had been moving along the Hebron road, making excursions to the east and west of the road. In this way he gained much practical knowledge of the strength of the enemy's forces, and particularly his defences on the north and the north-eastern sides. He was then making his way south on the eastern side of Beersheba. Both he and Jack, unknown to each other, were engaged in the same business of stalking the redoubt when they met, in the dramatic fashion already related.

They proceeded to make their investigations together. Taking advantage of the culpable carelessness of the Turks, they were able to climb the walls. Eid actually entered the stronghold and gained the exact information required. He located the guns.

There was no need now for Jack to proceed any farther. Eid was a most capable and trustworthy spy, and further, was in the pay and confidence of the British. He had in his possession the necessary particulars concerning the northern defences of Beersheba. These he freely communicated to Jack, offering shrewd criticisms the while. They now knew exactly what would have to be met with on the eastern side. Therefore it were wisdom to set out instantly on the homeward trek.

The return of the troop was uneventful. Keeping well to the eastward, they rode hard. Under Eid's direction, they arrived at a well before the day had far advanced, where was a supply of good drinking water. This was the only halt made during the day. They made the Wady Guzzeh by nightfall, and then, turning west, rode boldly through the dark, reaching Headquarters about three hours later.

Sir Harry was more than pleased when Jack and Eid had concluded their report. He now had the information that was lacking. By the aid of this and other reconnaissances, together with aerial photographs, he was in possession of highly important details touching all the enemy's positions. The extensive patrol work carried out during the months of organisation had familiarised the men with the character of the country over which they were to operate.

Before dismissing the two men, the general warmly complimented Jack upon the effectual and expeditious nature of his work. He had a flattering word at the same time for Eid. Before long the Commander-in-Chief was in full possession of the valuable details. These were of great assistance to the Staff in working out the minutiae of General Allenby's strategy.

The day had arrived. Months of ceaseless toil had brought the British, now strongly reinforced, to that condition of preparedness so essential to success. The undertaking was one of great magnitude. Under the direction of the Boches, the Turks had perfected their scheme of defence. Supposedly impregnable barriers barred the way of the British advance: of this the Turkish Headquarters Staff were assured by the self-confident Boche engineers. They awaited, therefore, with perfect equanimity the day when Britain should strike.

That the Turks, together with their arrogant allies, the Germans and Austrians, were outwitted and out-generalled soon became apparent. All through the months of preparation the British had the enemy guessing. Allenby's intention and organisation were shrouded in mystery impenetrable to his foes. Despite all their attempts to find out what was transpiring behind the British front, they gained little vital knowledge. They knew, it was true, something of the magnitude of the British Army and the composition of its units, but beyond that they remained in ignorance.

The British offensive opened in accordance with Moslem expectation. Greatly reinforced in artillery since our last reverse at Gaza, we made a furious bombardment of the Turkish lines in the coast sector. Guns of all calibre joined in a chorus of ear-splitting sounds infinitely greater, and a vomiting of lead much heavier, than had at any time been experienced in Palestine. The fire from the land batteries and from the warships was concentrated on Gaza and Alimuntar, which latter was an exceedingly strong position. The Turkish commanders, however, smiled at this demonstration of artillery force and waited for the infantry attack.

But the enemy only saw what the British willed him to

see. The commander at Beersheba, thirty miles away, had, as an act of precaution, sent out a strong force to make a reconnaissance. They had not proceeded far before they encountered a couple of Aussie squadrons. These inferior forces showed their mettle by holding the enemy off during the whole day. They were in the end compelled to make a temporary retirement, but by that time they had achieved their object. They had covered an infantry movement which was thereby enabled to proceed unobserved to a strong position, from which to attack the western defences of Beersheba. This column had marched all night, hiding in a wady during the succeeding day, and resuming their march behind the cavalry screen towards evening.

All Allenby's completed plans were now put into operation. His intention was to deliver a knockout blow at Beersheba while menacing Gaza by his artillery bombardment. The fall of Gaza would be consequent upon the capture of Beersheba.

All arms of the service participated in the carrying out of Allenby's strategy. It fell to the lot of the Anzac Cavalry —as the Australian Light Horse and the New Zealand Mounteds came now to be called—to take an important part in the great battle.

The story of the capture of Beersheba is the story of a splendidly planned movement, in which the infantry and cavalry combined, worked out with clock-like accuracy. The strength of its defences lay mostly on the western side, where the enemy had done everything possible to bar our approach. In their defensive preparations they were greatly assisted by Nature.

The task given to the infantry was an exceedingly tough one. They were to break through these strong barricades in the face of a murderous rain of shells and bullets. They would be called upon to storm hills that were miniature Gibraltars of impregnability. It was not intended to lay siege to them: they were to be captured by assault.

The splendid men of the Home counties and the

gallant Welsh were not to be held. No combination of the opposing forces could stay their rushes. They mounted the steep banks of wadies, tore down wire barricades with their hands, raced up fortified hills, and by a series of irresistible rushes broke down successive lines of defence. They incessantly stormed the enemy positions for twelve long hours, winning, at last, through the formidable Wady-Sanea system of trenches, and entered Beersheba on its western side as victors three hours after sunset.

Meanwhile other divisions had not been idle; and now the elaborate preparation for an extended movement bore fruit. For the great enveloping tactic mapped out for Chauvel's division, the ground had, as we have seen, been previously studied. Aerial observation and repeated cavalry reconnaissances had thoroughly familiarised the officers and men with the character of the work required of them and the nature of the obstacles to be overcome. Their particular part, a work of the highest importance, was to be carried out in a way that would dovetail in with the general plan. Sir Edmund Allenby's plan was worked out with meticulous care. In ideal it might be stated in the terms of an orchestra. Each piece of this combination of war-units was to contribute to the harmony of the whole. It is a matter of history that not one instrument in the great movement made a discordant note or fell below the ideal. The capture of Beersheba was in sober truth a triumph of Staff work.

The mobile forces, consisting of Australians, New Zealanders, and Yeomanry, moved out in order after sunset in the light of a lustrous moon. They were to carry out a great sweeping movement by which the Turkish position was to be outflanked. They rode through the night at a rapid pace, for time played an important part in the contract which they had accepted. Their immediate task was to "ring" the southern, eastern, and northern sides, leaving the west to the infantry. So Beersheba was to be bottled up and assaulted on all sides.

Every man engaged in this manoeuvre knew that there

would be little rest, except that which secrecy made a necessity, until the objectives were gained. Success now largely depended upon celerity and secrecy. Onward, through the night, sped men and horses, in no wild rush, but with a swiftness possible only to animals and men brought by their preparatory work to the pink of condition. The big-boned, muscular walers, inured to the conditions of desert travel, carried their riders with a springy stride that knew no abatement. They shared in the spirit of ecstasy which now filled the men in prospect of the fight which awaited them.

Sometimes riding hard, sometimes creeping through defiles, sometimes lying low, sometimes cutting off venturesome enemy patrols, the various positions were reached. So far no hitch had occurred. The men had done all they had been asked. The enemy, though now somewhat alarmed, had not taken in our general intention. His anxious attention was still concentrated on the coastal area, where the British artillery kept up an incessant fire. The Gaza defenders were no longer smiling. Their nerves were on the point of cracking, which was just the effect that Allenby was aiming to produce. Any lowering of the morale at any point would contribute to the eventual success of the whole. The Turkish Headquarters still believed that the big blow was to be delivered here, even up to the moment when, thirty miles to the east, the carefully prepared assault was on the eve of being launched.

When the Turkish commander at Beersheba did wake up to the fact, it was too late. His lines of communication to the west and north had been cut, and he had to prepare as best he could to stay the onrush that would take no denial.

The regiment in which the Eureka Amalgamateds served was attached to the brigade which held a position on the north-east. Their immediate objective was a high hill, strongly defended, which dominated a wide area. This must be taken before the Hebron road could be cut, and there was no time to be wasted. The way in which the Aussies passed over the wide, bare, bullet-swept plateau at top speed, fought their way to the crest of the hill, and drove the surprised Jackoes out of their holes and from behind their barricades, was an object-lesson in open fighting.

That piece of work done to the satisfaction of all concerned, a regiment was ordered to seize the northern road, and so completely seal the town.

But now a formidable barrier of trenches, flanked with redoubts, interposed between the Light Horse and Beersheba. In this system the outpost which Jack and Eid had stalked on a memorable evening not long before was conspicuous. Its position was naturally strong, being almost encircled by the steep banks of a wady. But the obstacles, however formidable, were surmounted by clever approach and swift rushes. The Anzacs, who had scaled the precipitous slopes of Gallipoli, were not to be daunted by height, nor depth, nor any other barrier that the Turk might put in their way.

The particulars furnished by Jack to General Chauvel made their task the easier. The youthful colonel led the way to the weakest point of the redoubt, and in a few minutes the New Zealanders and the Aussies were swarming over the walls. The Turks were overwhelmed after a brief struggle, and surrendered in hundreds.

But there were other posts to take before the final assault could be made. Nests of German machine-gunners had to be routed, and the whole face on the north-east and east cleared, before entering upon the last stage.

It was now nightfall. Both men and horses had been without water for thirty hours. Yet, though lolling tongues hung from between parched lips, and the torment of an insatiate thirst ravished man and beast, the word of command was still "Carry on!"

Despite the handicap of a devouring thirst, the fire of battle burned fiercely in each Light Horseman's breast. And now the supreme moment has come. Beyond yonder bristling line of defences lies victory! Over yonder, too, lies that which at this moment is more alluring than the prospect of victory—a deep draught from the well of Abraham!

"General Grant's brigade will attack!"

So ran the order from the divisional chief. The way in which that order was carried out constitutes the most brilliant episode in the battle of Beersheba. Gathering his men together in open formation, the brigadier gave the astonishing order: "Fix bayonets!" Then: "Charge!"

Forgotten in a moment were fatigue and thirst. Filled with the joy of battle, the squadrons raced to the charge through the moonlit night. Using their bayonets as lances, they literally swept over all opposition. Line after line was taken with breathless haste. The Turks, fear-stricken, fled at last before the terrific onrush of the dreadful Giaours.

On swept the brigade, the other Anzacs rattling at their heels. A final attempt to rally was broken, and the conquering bands galloped into the town.

Here confusion indescribable reigned. Almost simultaneously with the Aussies' entrance on the eastern, came the Tommies' on the western side of the town, the latter having, as related, broken down all opposition. English, Irish, Scotch, Australian, New Zealander, participated in the mix-up. Rifle and revolver fire came from every direction, and pandemonium reigned for a while. The clean-up, however, was expeditiously carried out, and in a short time all opposition was silenced; the last resistance offered came from the vicinity of the wells.

So great was the surprise of the final night charge that the enemy had not been able to do much damage to the place before flying or surrendering. Beyond one or two wrecking explosions, the place was undamaged. So unexpected was the capture that the warehouses were full of corn and other military supplies. A train ready to start was still standing at the station.

All this work had not been carried out without many casualties. Many a brave Tommy, Aussie, and Maorilander died in the hour of victory. May we not say of these lads, as was said of one who died on a kopje crest in South Africa:

> "He hath lived much—for all he lived not long—
>   For he hath realised in one brief strife
> Such pulse and flame and sacrifice and song
>   As none may know who live to save their life."

The ambulance corps had worked hard all through the day. While many of the fighters could now get some respite, the rescuers and doctors carried on throughout the night without a moment's rest. The tents were soon overflowing with cases. All night the wounded were being brought in in a ceaseless stream, and many hours would pass ere the surgeon's knife would be laid down.

The padres, where not ministering to the dying, doffed tunics, and did a shift at stretcher-bearing.

CHAPTER XXIII

HOW GAZA FELL AND HOW THE GREAT DRIVE
OPENED

THE capture of Beersheba was a fine piece of work, both in its planning and execution. The brain that conceived it, and the various branches of arms which executed it, alike shared in the brilliance of the great exploit; for, while it will go down in history as a triumph of Allenby's strategy, it will at the same time be a monument of the magnificence of his troops. No section of his command held a monopoly of efficiency and heroic bearing. Nor were they old soldiers, reckoned by years, who won the tough Turkish stronghold. They were young men—youths in whom the spirit of the old crusaders dwelt, inspiring them in battle to the point of a splendid audacity that laughed at impossibilities, and at the same time created a disdain of the well-worn methods of attack. They were true successors to Richard the Lion Heart.

The capture of Beersheba was only one point in Sir Edmund Allenby's game. The bombardment of Gaza continued uninterruptedly. Night and day for many days an everflowing stream of lead and steel fell upon the elaborate trench systems. Naval guns and field artillery belched forth their murderous projectiles, subjecting the Turks to a gun-assault that was beyond all their previous experiences in intensity and weight.

"The British take Gaza.? Never!" shouted Jacko and Boche in contemptuous laughter, when the storm burst. But as day succeeded day, and still the stream of high explosives and shrapnel continued, battering his redoubts and communication trenches, searching out his hidden guns and rendering them useless, taking a heavy toll of his fighters the while, small wonder that the Turk lost his *morale* and yielded to panic.

When, finally, our troops were ordered to attack this impregnable stronghold, they in turn were surprised. Instead of a formidable and bloody hand-to-hand tussle in the trenches, it was little more than a walk-over. It was almost unbelievable that such a place should be yielded without a serious scrap, for the trenches were unusually deep and well-protected, and the dug-outs were quite elaborate, roofed in with tree-trunks and sand-bags. The material of the latter showed a curious combination of cotton, silk, and wool, being dress materials of various sorts which had been requisitioned in the usual fashion from the native population.

There were places, it is true, where the Turks made a stand and even met with temporary success. At Knwfeslhe Ridge, for instance, on the right flank, where the gallant Welsh and the English county troops attacked, Jacko put up a stiff fight. He even attempted to outflank us. Here several of his strong divisions were located, and he was well led. It was, however, a vain endeavour to retrieve the disaster which had overtaken the general body of his troops. The British were not to be denied. After a partial retirement under great pressure they came again, and this time the Moslem battalions broke and fled northward.

Meanwhile, the enemy holding the Kaauwakah system, farther east, was ejected from his position. He took refuge in some broken country north of Sheria, and in turn threatened the British flank. But the Yeomanry were too much for him.

And now there remained of the original lines of defence, stretching from Gaza to Beersheba, only Attawines. This, it is true, was a tough problem, being an immensely strong sector of the system. It was not to be carried by assault until it had first been reduced by bombardment. So a heavy gunfire was let loose upon it. The Turks, after a brave resistance, concluded that retreat was justifiable under the circumstances. They were urged to this by two considerations. They were being decimated by a merciless gunfire; and they were cut off from support, both on the right and left. In a short time they would be completely surrounded. Who will blame them for taking "leg bail"?

Within ten days of the initial movement of Allenby's troops for the capture of Beersheba, the whole system of Turkish defence, twenty miles long, stretching between the two strongly-fortified bases of Gaza and Beersheba, was demolished.

Not a single post along the east-west line remained in Turkish hands. Despite his elaborate systems, which were the last word in German technical skill, his divisions were driven out of cover. Minus many thousands in killed, wounded, and prisoners, they were now flying northward in great confusion before the exultant British.

That the enemy was out-generalled was self-evident. In strategy he was easily beaten on points. Yet strategy was not the only factor that contributed to the British success. The Turk was beaten by a more ardent spirit. That, more than any artifice of war, drove him pell-mell from his redoubts and barricades. Here was the secret of the British triumphs: her unkillable spirit. This never deserts her in adversity, and survives defeat, ever rising from its ashes to victory. No student of English history can have failed to mark this trait, and the Great War has shown, on the Marne, on the Tigris, and on the Wady Guzzeh, the self-same spirit in the British of all types gathered together from the far-flung dominions of the Empire.

"Shure, Misther Jack, ye'll have to go in the officers' ward for a few days, an' give your wounds a chance."

"What?—Me? Not on your life, my boy. Got something better to do than to loaf in a hospital tent."

"But ye're not fit to—!"

"Get out, you old mollycoddle! Slept like a top in a railway carriage last night. Ate like a horse this morning.

And now you've bandaged up these scratches I'm as fit as a fiddle. To tell you the truth, I didn't know I'd been wounded until I woke up this morning."

"I wish, Major, ye'd see the docther about your leg. He'd —"

"Order me to roost. I know. No surgeons for me, Tim. The brigade's off in an hour. Our lot go out in advance. Got to keep the beggars on the run, you know. It's going to be hammer and tongs. As soon as Gaza falls we're going to sweep up Philistia. That'll be some going, old fellow. It'll be for all the world like a great kangaroo drive."

"Well, Major dear, ye'll have your own way as usual. Please take this bottle of iodine an' this little packet of bandages. It's that leg I'm worried about. The muscle's terribly bruised. Ye're shurely not fit for the saddle."

"It looks a jolly sight worse than it feels. The liniment'll soon take all the sting out of it. By George, Tim! 'Tis the lucky man I am to have got through so well. Our regiment, as you know, was in the thick of it all through the scrap. So was the brigade, for that matter. The brigadier's made a great name for himself."

"What is it?" cried he, breaking off his speech with Tim and turning to an orderly who stood at attention.

"General Grant says he wants to see you immediately, sir."

"Righto. Good-bye, Tim. Oh yes, I'll smother the scratches with iodine."

Jack Smith was not the soldier to take his wounds seriously, especially in prospect of the great advance which was imminent. For this they had been preparing through the weary months. That which had especially fired their imagination was the deliverance of Jerusalem from Moslem misrule. Though taken individually Johnny Turk was not half so bad as he had been painted, taken collectively and as a ruler, he deserved all the execration heaped upon him. To drive him out of Southern Palestine and capture Jerusalem was the fond dream of every British soldier, from the C.-i.-C. to the lowest and rawest ranker.

Jack limped along to Brigade Headquarters, feeling more pain than he acknowledged to his old mate, Sergeant Hogan. He was thankful that no bones were broken, and felt confident that his slight wounds would prove no obstacle to the performance of his present duties.

But a shock was awaiting Jack the moment he stood before the brigadier.

"Good morning, General," said he at the salute.

"Morning, Colonel. Hearty congrats."

"'Colonel'? 'Congratulations'? I—I don't know what you mean, General. What joke's this you're putting up on me?"

"Look here, Smith, joking's off in this case. It's solid and dinkum," laughed the brigadier, as he quizzed Jack's puzzled face.

"But, a—?"

"No butter about it. Plenty of hard graft, you young dog. Your colonel's appointed to Staff work, and will likely get a brigade as soon as there's a vacancy. Oh, no need to thank me. It's due to you, my boy. I was glad to put in a word for you. Not that it was necessary. No one's better pleased than myself, and here's my hand on it. It's brevet rank, you understand?"

"Thank you, sir. I'm sure I don't deserve it."

"Cut that out, Smith. You don't get it by favour."

"Who's taking my place, sir?"

"Whom do you think?"

"I know who I'd clearly like to get it, not simply on the ground of friendship, but on the ground of sterling worth."

"Who's that?"

"Captain Mackenzie, sir, of B troop."

"Your old friend, eh?"

At this instant Jock Mackenzie made his appearance at the tent opening.

"Good morning, Major Mackenzie," said the brigadier, with an accent on the title, while a merry twinkle appeared in his eyes.

"Captain, sir," said Jock in some wonderment, as he looked at the laughing faces of the brigadier and Smith. "It's my friend here that's the major."

"That's where you make a mistake, my boy. Your 'friend here,' as you put it, is no longer major. You must address him with all due respect as colonel."

"W—well, if this doesn't beat cockfighting!" cried the amazed lad as the truth broke in upon him. They had both received promotion! For the moment he hardly thought of his own rise in his joy at Jack's elevation. Without another word he stepped up to the "Sanior Partner of the Eureka Amalgamateds," as Tim Hogan persisted in calling the late major, and wrung his hand with much fervency. This was returned with equal strength.

"Well, now, gentlemen, to business!" exclaimed General Grant. "Colonel Smith, you'll take charge of your command immediately and proceed along the Hebron road. Your business will be to observe the enemy's movements. My latest information is that he is disposed to make a stand in the high ground. Sir Harry wants definite information, and a judgment formed on the spot as to the likelihood of the Turks making a counter-attack. If so, we shall have to concentrate."

"I understand, sir. This is to be a reconnaissance and not a demonstration?"

"That's about it. We don't want to attack in force until General Allenby's ready for a general advance."

"I understand, sir."

"Well, now, be off with you," said Grant in a genial manner.

"Hello, Colonel!" exclaimed he the next moment, as that officer was limping out of the bivvy. "Is that a wooden leg you've manufactured?"

"No, sir," replied Jack, with a hearty laugh. "Nothing so bad us that. Spent bullet or bit of shell bruised my thigh. I'll be all right in the saddle."

"Well, take care of yourself, and report to me the moment you've made your observations."

With a final salute Jack and Jock passed away from the Brigade Headquarters.

"Well, Major! How do you feel about it all?" exclaimed Jack to Jock after a moment's silence.

"Feel? That's just it, old man. I feel like a blushing bride at the wedding feast when her new title's boasted. How are you feeling yourself, if it comes to that?"

"Feeling ? Why, not ten minutes ago old Tim Hogan was urging me at the dressing station to go into hospital and lay up for a spell. Yet, here I am, swaggering along, 'Colonel Smith,' if you please; ordered to conduct an immediate stunt. Blest if I won't have to cultivate a fierce moustache to live up to it!"

Before midday Jack had gathered his men together, a sadly depleted regiment, and moved out to the execution of the order. When the officers and men were apprised of his promotion they showered congratulations upon him. Mackenzie, too, came in for his full share. The men felt that the two pals were one with themselves. It was a true *camaraderie*, and in no way interfered with the discipline of the regiment. Officers of this type get the most out of their men.

Proceeding cautiously, the regiment moved in the direction where they might gain the completest information of the defeated enemy. As they proceeded onward they began to realise how great had been the panic of the enemy. Those who had escaped before the ring of the enveloping horsemen was made complete had retired in the greatest confusion. The branching tracks contiguous to the main road, as well as the road itself, were littered with dead horses and bullocks. Transport vehicles were broken and overturned. Machine-guns and ammunition of all sorts had been thrown aside in the wild rush.

After proceeding for some distance the column encountered some rough country, with hills, here and there, rising a few hundreds of feet high. These were carefully explored and a few captures made—principally snipers. Jack's fear was that machine-gun sections might be planted in some of the elevated positions which lent themselves to nests of that character.

He was greatly relieved to find, after proceeding some

distance through this class of country, that nothing of that nature was to be apprehended. The retreat, according to all the signs, had been general. For all these assurances, he was not leaving anything to chance. His advance was on the slow side, because his survey was thorough. It covered a wide front when the strength of the column is considered.

Moving in this deliberate yet thorough way, he arrived at a wady crossing. Here, in the riverbed, was a 5-inch gun and limber, together with several overturned waggons and a number of dead animals. This *débris* quite blocked the crossing for any vehicular traffic.

"I say, sir," exclaimed M'Thirst, who was now a senior sergeant in Jack's regiment, "this is a pretty mess, isn't it? Wonder where the shell that did it came from?"

"Do you see the peak of that hill about a couple of miles to the east, Sergeant?"

Following his colonel's index finger, Sergeant M'Thirst saw the crest of a hill which rose above all intervening objects.

"Yes, Colonel, I see."

"You observe it commands this crossing?"

"That is so, sir."

"Would it surprise you to know that a British battery has been established somewhere on that hill?"

"Not if you say so, sir. Can't see any sign, though. Blame me, but it's cleverly concealed."

"It's there all right. At any rate, it was there last night. We occupied the hill at midday. Here's some work for our engineers. Corporal Brown, you'll return to Headquarters and report on the condition of this spot at once. The sooner the engineers get on the job the better. The crossing must be made practicable for our forward movement. Tell General Grant the country's quite safe up to this point."

Crossing the wady, the column turned due north and made its way for some distance without coming in touch with the enemy. They were now several miles distant from

Beersheba. So far there was no sign that the enemy had decided to make a stand with the object of counter-attacking. While they were proceeding across a level piece of country, the well-known hum of an advancing aeroplane became audible. Eagerly scanning the sky in the direction of the sound, one of the men suddenly cried, "Here she comes!"

The taube was now distinctly visible. It had emerged from behind a belt of clouds to the north, and was bearing down directly upon the horsemen.

"Scatter!"

It hardly needed the colonel's command for the men to separate in all directions. By this manoeuvre, rapidly executed, no target was left to the enemy. Nothing much was to be feared unless one was unlucky enough to be struck by a flying fragment of bomb. The firing, however, was not all on the one side. The men opened a fierce fusillade upon the low-flying machine, which almost immediately took flight to avoid the rattling bullets.

The reconnaissance proceeded until nightfall. During the late afternoon the advanced scouts surprised a big motor-lorry on which were a dozen men, including a German major and captain. The lorry was travelling leisurely along a narrow valley, where was the only practicable road. M'Thirst, who was in the advance with half a dozen men, made a short *détour* as soon as the lorry was sighted. Galloping round a ridge unseen by the occupants, he cut the road a hundred yards ahead of the travellers. So quietly was this movement made that the enemy had no thought of danger until they saw a group of Aussies a short distance ahead, barring the way. In the meantime another section of men came down on the road behind them and so cut off their retreat.

In obedience to a rapid order, the driver drove the lorry at full speed ahead. He had not gone twenty yards before he fell from his seat, with a bullet through his brain. M'Thirst rarely made a miss. The immediate result of the shot, apart from the death of the driver, was the overturning of the vehicle.

The rage of the Boche major was beyond description. Cursing and frothing at the mouth, he scrambled to his feet, pulled out his revolver to fire point-blank at M'Thirst, who was approaching him. He lingered just a fraction too long in pulling the trigger. Jack arrived on the scene just in time to anticipate the act, saving his sergeant from a certain death by drilling a hole through the officer's heart ere he could bring the necessary pressure on the trigger. There was no trouble with the others.

Night had now fallen, and the purpose of the reconnaissance having been achieved, the regiment started on its return.

CHAPTER XXIV

HOW THE AUSSIES KEPT IN THE VAN, AND HOW THE SCOTS MADE GOOD

THE victorious British were now pressing the Turks along a line which stretched across the maritime plain, turning their retreat in many places into a rout. Large numbers of the enemy were pushing along the Hebron road towards Jerusalem and the western defences, but for the most part they clung to the old Philistinian routes.

General Allenby was determined to give the enemy no rest. In this he was ably backed by his men. Every man, from the highest to the lowest, was extended to the utmost in the pursuit. The Turks showed a peculiar aptitude for scattering. A covey of flushed quail or a brood of wild ducklings were hardly in it with Abdul, Hassan and Company when they assumed the role of a quitter.

In the rounding-up process the Aussies were in their element; it was a game of which thousands of them knew all the points. It recalled to many their cattle-station days and the periodic drives, when, mounted on their stock-horses, stock-whip in hand, they raked the gullies and combed out the scrubs, ringing the big mobs of half-wild cattle to the musketry of whip-crackings. Yes, "Yaller" Billy, Bobnawarra Mac, Thargomindah Frank, Barcoo Bob, and many another of that class, were having the time of their life, as they pursued the Jackoes in the hill country of Judea, driving them out of their hiding-places like slinking dingoes, or following them up the dry wadies and across the sand-dimes on the left flank.

The work of the pursuing columns at this stage was not rendered any easier by climatic conditions. The rainy season was long overdue. The heat was intolerable. Clouds of dust assaulted mouths, noses, and eyes in an irritating fashion. The drive was conducted across waterless country. Consequently Nature imposed a heavy strain upon both men and horses. All honour to the transport units. In doing their utmost to mitigate the sufferings of men and animals they performed prodigies. Motor lorries provided with large tanks, and camels bearing loads of provender and rations, followed up the advance, wrestling with the execrable roads, oftentimes having to construct a road as they moved along. The motors, in the long run, had to be abandoned, and the brunt of the work fell on the camel transport service. It often happened, however, in the experience of the impetuous horsemen, that they rode and fought for thirty and forty hours in the burning heat, without the opportunity of slaking their thirst or resting their weary bodies. Still, in spite of every obstacle, nothing daunted their exultant spirits.

It was the fortune of the "Eureka Amalgamateds" to occupy a position on the left of the drive, and on the left wing of the Light Horse Division. This brought them into touch with the English. The latter were pushing along the coastal sand-dunes, and had now reached a point on the Wady Hesy. Farther east they advanced on Huj, which they captured in a brilliant fashion, taking a quantity of guns and other munitions. This exploit was performed by the Warwickshire and the Worcestershire Yeomanry. On the same day the Imperial Cavalry (Indian) captured Beit Hanum, the railhead of the Gaza branch of the railway. Here large stores of booty fell into our hands.

The Aussies, it is safe to say, were not missing their opportunities. The brigade to which our lads were attached was sometimes supporting the infantry and yeomanry, and at others conducting an independent drive, knocking the heels of the retreating enemy and cutting out batches of men. This was not without resistance. Occasionally considerable bodies, holding strong, natural positions, would stand at bay. But nothing could hold the Light Horse. Resistance was all in the game. The exciting moments in a bovine round-up used to come when some half-maddened beast would charge, with as little consideration as a Malay running amuck, or when a mob of hard-pressed cattle made an attempt to break through the ring of the enveloping stockmen, and gallop back to their haunts in the scrubs and gullies. It was on such occasions that the cattleman was at his best. So, now, in the greater drive, when the hotly-pressed enemy called halt and counter-attacked, the military stockmen adopted instinctively their bush tactics. Thereupon the spurt of the enemy faded quickly away, smothered by the converging rush of the wide-spread pursuers.

After crossing the Wady Hesy the going became easier; therefore the advance was more rapid. This, of course, meant that the flight of the Turks was accelerated. So bent were they upon saving their skins that they gave no thought to anything or to anyone outside their individual selves. The result of this to the native population was beneficial. The Turk, at this stage, had no time even for pillage. To the north of the Hesy the villages became more numerous, which was all to our advantage.

It is easy to understand how a people who had been under the dead hand of the Turk for generations, during which they had suffered many personal cruelties, having been kept on the border-line of starvation by iniquitous taxes, would turn gratefully to their deliverers. News had, during the past few months, filtered up from the south, which put the Antipodeans in a more favourable light: the treatment of the people in the captured towns of El Arish and Rafa, to wit. This had been exactly opposite to that which they were led to expect by their masters, should the terrible baby-eating Giaours win. Their eyes were now opening to the advantages of a new rule, wherein justice and humanity were more than mere names. The Arab communities were now more than willing to welcome the British, infidels though they were, as a blessing from Allah.

Jack's regiment, which was in advance of the brigade,

acting as a leading patrol, occupied a large Arab village about midday. As they jogged wearily through the main street of the village the people rushed out from their mud huts in joyous acclaim. An hour or so previously a ragged battalion of Turkish infantry had passed through in the utmost disorder. Not half the men were armed, their weapons having been thrown aside to lighten their burdens. All discipline seemed to have been abandoned. Had they had some leisure moments they were ripe for mischief. But time was of the utmost value. Their officers were all in the van of the retreat, looking out for number one, selfishly leaving their men to their own devices. There was no rearguard. The officers' example was infectious. Every man acted on the principle of the devil taking the hindmost.

Had they not been in a veritable panic they would, in all likelihood, have vented their feelings upon the unoffending villagers in no tender fashion. But such was their hurry—for those in the rear had caught a glimpse of a party of Aussie scouts back a space—that they passed through at the double without a halt.

The plight of their whilom masters, which showed defeat in its every phase, confirmed the rumours which had reached the Arabs' ears of the capture of their strongholds in the south by the British. These masters of swagger of arrogance were, after all, no better than dogs. Like the village mongrels, they were fleeing before the assault with their tails between their legs. Allah had been moved at last to requite these faithless followers of the great Prophet!

As soon as the regiment had passed through the village, Jack called a halt. There are limits to human endurance, even when the powers of mind and body have been keyed by the tonic of victory to the highest pitch. The limit had been reached hours ago. Both men and horses had dropped out. Save when in touch with the enemy, their movements were mechanical and their expressions wooden.

Having satisfied himself that the village did not contain a trap, and that the smiling faces of the villagers were not to be viewed as a mask for some mischievous intention worked by the slim Turks, Jack resolved to camp his regiment long enough for them to get some hours' sleep.

They had so harried the enemy that little immediate danger was to be apprehended from him. He was not going to strike back at the present stage. On the other hand, rest and sleep were essential to a further vigorous pursuit.

He drew up his men at the outskirts of the village common. The country round about was fertile, and the villagers were not Bedouins. They took some pains in the cultivation of their gardens, and surrounding the town were fruit and vegetable gardens.

Having seen to his men, who were watering their steeds at the wells, he sent a squad along the road some little distance as a precaution against surprise. Then, calling one of the villagers, who were now mingling fearlessly with the men, offering them quantities of fruit, he ordered him to lead him to the sheikh. This did not take many minutes, and in due course he was in the presence of the alcade. This person was a long-haired and full-bearded Arab, robed in Eastern magnificence, in which the picturesque took upon itself the character of the tawdry.

The old man had got himself up in anticipation of such a visit, and was bent on producing an unmistakable impression of his importance. Jack sensed his object, and while he humoured it to some extent, he soon gave the gentleman to understand in plain Arabic that, while the British were ready to be true friends to the native inhabitants, according them perfect freedom in their religious belief and industrial pursuits, any overt act resembling treachery would be visited with severe punishment.

The alcade had nous enough to see that the British officer was not bluffing, and would be prepared to back up

"In due course he was in the presence of the Alcade."

his statements. To tell the truth, the old man was in his heart glad to think that the days of misrule were over.

No one, whether Eastern or Western, could be long in Jack's company without being alive to the sense of his personality, and the alcade was no exception. The young colonel had hardly made his statement before the old fellow was salaaming and smiling, exuding benevolence and goodwill, as it were, from every pore of his animated countenance.

He swore by Allah and Mahomet that his own grave and those of his innumerable ancestors might be for ever defiled should he now or at any time in the future give sanction to any other act than that of good-fellowship. All this, and much more that was eulogistic of the conquerors, was poured forth like water from a sluice. All the flowers of the East were made into a bouquet of words and placed before the youthful colonel for his acceptance.

Jack, by this time, was pretty well used to Eastern blarney. His enforced residence with the Bedouins, as well as his contact with the various types in Egypt, had familiarised him with the expansive compliments which might mean anything or nothing. In the present instance, while not disposed to take every utterance of the alcade's mealy-mouthed protestations at its face value, he felt sure that the old gentleman was unfeigned in his delight at the change of masters, and hoped that it might be made permanent. He trusted the alcade to appreciate the buttered side of his bread.

Passing along the street in Jack's company, he called aloud to his people to show the conquering heroes every consideration, and bestow their fruits and their goods upon them without money and without price. This they did without stint. Nevertheless they did not refuse payment when it was offered. To do so would have been putting too great a strain on their generous instincts, which had never before been so taxed.

It will be readily understood that Billjim Aussie was not carrying much cash about with him during the great drive. For the most part, he was moneyless. Therefore the free, gratis, and for nothing order of the alcade was of the utmost service. The soldiers were nothing loath to become pensioners on the Arabs' bounty. The succulent orange and the appetising if pungent garlic gave variety to their strictly limited *menu*.

The men could hardly keep awake to the finish of their meal. Many, indeed, were so worn that they flung themselves on the sward, risking the chance of tucker when they should be awakened. Before long, with the exception of the few on guard, the whole regiment was in profound slumber.

During this interval Jack and Jock kept watch and watch, to use a nautical phrase. The guard, too, was changed, so that most of the men had six hours' solid sleep. The horses lay at full length along the lines.

The camp was aroused at sundown. Men and horses were fed and watered. "Boot and saddle" was then sounded, and the column resumed its march. By this time the brigade, which had halted earlier, was in touch with its advanced section.

Acting in concert with the Yeomanry, who were performing daring deeds, the Anzac Cavalry Division advanced over a wide area. Askelon, which was an old crusading town, though little even of its ruins remains, was speedily captured, and the harried Turks were forced back to Ashdod. After a short fight Ashdod was ours.

The Light Horse Brigade, in whose deeds we are more nearly concerned, moved northward, inclining towards the east. Their immediate objective was El Tineh, situated on the railway line at the point where the Gaza-Jerusalem and the Beersheba-Jerusalem lines junction. This was considered an important base, where large stores of munitions and food were held.

The Turks holding this place were in an extremely nervous condition. When it became evident that the British were sweeping northward like an irresistible tidal wave, they were seized with funk. Even should they succeed in holding the enemy oil in their particular locality, they would be cut off from all support by the advance of the invading line elsewhere. There was nothing to be gained and everything to be lost by holding on, and the garrison had no mind to be marooned. But the stores! Well, one thing was certain: they could not be removed. Time was the essence of this contract, and the removal of the stores would occupy many days. There was no time for removal; but what could not be removed could and would be burned.

The work of destruction was begun with the utmost expedition, but before the numerous fires had got well alight the Turks were engaged in a hot running fight with the Light Horse. After a stilt tussle, those who were not killed or taken prisoner were fleeing northward. The troopers were just in time to save large quantities of booty.

So northward the tide of battle rolled, up the main coastal way through heavy sand-dunes on the left flank; along the Hebron road on the extreme right flank; and on both sides of the railway line in the centre.

Jack's regiment was now in the vicinity of El Shargish, which is the modern name for ancient Gath. The ground they were covering was steeped in history of absorbing interest. Gath, of course, was the home of Goliath, the giant and champion of the Philistines when they met the Israelites in battle in the valley of Elah. There, on one of the affluents of the Wady Surah, did young David the Bethlehemite shepherd-boy take up the taunting challenge issued by the great warrior, and bring the mountainous body of the boaster to earth with a well-placed pebble.

Hereabouts was Ekron, the seat of the god Beelzebub, the god of flies. Singular to relate, the Aussies encountered a horde of flies in this district, out of all proportion to what they had hitherto experienced. Every well and every village and every hill in this region is reminiscent of persons and deeds figuring in Old Testament history. Gath, of which mention has been made, is associated with more modern history. It was taken and held by the crusaders, notably King Richard and the Knights Templar. Of the five old Philistine towns which played so important a part during the crusades,—Ashdod, Askelon, Gaza, Gath, and Ekron,—only Ekron (now called Akir) remained at this stage in the possession of the Turks. And it was soon to pass away from them.

It was fully expected that the Turks would make a decided stand along the Wady Surah. The wady made an extremely good line of defence.

A resolute foe could make things tremendously hard for the pursuers. The chances of a successful defence were good. But it was not taken advantage of. The commanders had, for the most part, lost touch with their men. Certain rallying-points, it is true, were held, and stiff local fights were put up here and there. But, generally speaking, the units had lost cohesion, and were utterly dispirited. The overthrow of the southern barriers was so complete, and the "follow on" policy of Sir Edmund Allenby so rapid, that there was no chance of reinforcements from northern Palestine arriving in time to check the victorious British legions.

Within a few days of the fall of Gaza, the Anzac Cavalry and the Yeomanry had forced a crossing at the Wady Surah. From thence they swooped upon Junction Station, on the main line to Jerusalem.

Let it not for a moment be thought that the chief glory and honour of the advance belongs to the Mounteds, whether Australian, New Zealander, or Yeomanry. They had, it is true, the advantage of greater mobility, but held no monopoly of daring or resource.

The exploits of the Scots, for instance, stand on a level with any feat performed by our troops in Palestine. For advancing under enormous difficulties, overcoming all obstacles, taking hard knocks and giving knock-out blows, they were not a whit behind the very chiefest of the Anzacs. When the "Deeds that won Jerusalem" are committed to paper, their record will be among the most lustrous.

It was the Scottish battalions which stormed and captured the immensely strong positions of Umbrella Hill and El Arish Redoubt, in the vicinity of Gaza, during the first stage of Allenby's operations. With thinned ranks they marched northwards on the left flank, in company with the Berkshires, the Warwickshires, and other English battalions. The way for the first twenty miles or so over the heavy sand-dunes would have greatly fatigued the ordinary mortal, unencumbered by any weight. When the marching kit is taken into consideration it will be readily understood how great the handicap was. But, to make matters worse, the loose sand proved to be too much for the horses attached to the artillery train. The guns had frequently to be handled by the men. In all this, haste had to be kept in mind, lest they should lose touch with the flying foe, whose line of retreat showed his hurry, by the quantity of *impedimenta* which strewed the way.

It was full dark when they reached the bank of the Wady Hesy. Had prudence been the guiding star of these sons of Scotland they would have camped on the south side rather than have risked the passage of the wady in the darkness. But, though knowing full well that the north bank was held by the enemy in force, they joyfully crossed over, rushed the ridges in the vicinity, where the Turks had elected to take their stand, and drove them from their positions at the point of the bayonet.

Hand in hand with the Yeomanry and other mounted units, they chased the quarry. Askelon was quickly seized, and when the Mounteds had reached Ashdod the Scots were close behind. The town was taken in a stride by the Yeomanry, but the Turks held the ridges to the north, commanding the watering-place. From these coigns of vantage they covered the watering-place, making it impossible for the famished troopers to get a drink, or supply their horses.

But the indomitable Scots had now arrived. Without pause for rest or drink, they were formed up and went forward at the double in the darkness, this being their third night attack within four days. Needless to say, Jacko was quite ready to quit and to continue his northerly retreat after a further short experience of Scotty's bayonet.

But there was much yet to be done before the Scotsmen could call a halt. North of Ashdod, some eight or nine miles, lay Burkah.

Here the enemy had constructed two lines of trenches, with glacis slopes. They had also strong artillery support. The positions were taken after a stem hand-to-hand fight. In this those born fighters, the merry little Gurkhas, co-operated.

Then came Katrah, where the Scots' companions-in-arms were the Yeomanry, who performed brilliantly.

The Turks made sure of turning the tide of battle at Katrah. Everything was in their favour there; but once again they were turned out of their positions. The Scots advanced in the open as steadily as though on parade. While they so advanced, the gallant Yeomanry crossed the plain and galloped to the hills at the rear of the enemy. Then, dismounting, they closed in on him. This manoeuvre distracted his attention, and while so exercised the Scots rushed the position. Beset before and behind, the Turks, though they put up a good fight, soon realised that they were in a cleft stick, and surrendered. A splendid haul of 1400 prisoners, three field guns, and twenty-eight machine-guns was made.

The next day the Scots joined up with the Aussies and others, driving the enemy with ease, and reached the Jerusalem line by evening. This was the seventh day of the drive, during which they had marched nearly seventy miles in a zigzag line, with engagements along the whole way at short intervals.

When it is remembered that all this marching and fighting took place in blinding heat, and often across waterless tracts, the character of the exploit is heightened. They were all at it and always at it for that never-to-be-forgotten seven days. There was no grumbling and no malingering. This is also true of all the units of Allenby's army, whether English, Welsh, Irish, Anzacs, or Indians. It has been a common saying with the Aussies ever since the Great Drive, "The Tommies are good enough for me." This idiom from an Australian is the highest form of praise.

The whole army, in short, was keyed up to the highest point of endurance. They were infected, from the highest to the lowest, with the crusading spirit. They were the Army of Deliverance, and the Holy Land, held in vile thrall for so many centuries, to the grief of Christendom, was to be freed through their instrumentality.

They had advanced from Egypt, fighting their way along every yard of the distance. Checked at times, but never defeated in its supreme purpose, this army, made up of men drawn from the two ends of the earth, steadily clove its way upward and prevailed against all the odds of a determined foe, unsparing heat, blistering drought, and transport problems, in a desert country which had defeated the mighty Napoleon. Now, at last, it has driven the enemy in its strength from its strongholds in southern Palestine, up along the maritime plain, back over the Judean hills, until its strong lines of pursuit stretch from Jaffa on the sea-coast to Hebron in the very heart of Judea.

Was it not too good to be true'? Within a short fortnight of the opening shot of the offensive, the enemy, consisting of nine divisions, having a choice of situation, holding an apparently impregnable line, buttressed in strategy and defensive operations by picked brains from Germany and Austria, abundantly supplied with guns of heavy and light calibre, and a sufficiency of munitions and food, had been driven with violence from its fortifications and trenches and forced into a general retreat, which had become a rout in many places. Day after day and night after night he fled before the pursuit, until at last, weary, dispirited, and utterly demoralised, abandoning all hope of a final stand at the Surah River, he took refuge in the high, precipitous hills to the west and north-west of Jerusalem, which constitute the great natural defences of the Holy City.

But the tale of the capture of Lydda, Ramleh, and Jaffa, in which our young friends took a share, has yet to be told. Once the Junction Station was in our hands we made rapid progress northward. The mobile forces swept village and town until El Ramleh was reached. The troopers had simply romped over the rich, fertile tracts, being hailed everywhere by the inhabitants as veritable saviours. Compared with what the Light Horse had just passed through, the present experience was quite a picnic. The harried Turk at this stage nowhere stood upon the ceremony of his going. The first glimpse of the pursuit set all his nerves a-jangle and automatically sped his legs in flight.

The Turks were preparing to retire from Ramleh as an advanced squadron sighted the town. A sharp scrap took place in the environs, in which they were worsted, and then the victors clattered up the cobbled streets. There was no mistaking their reception. The whole population welcomed them with unfeigned joy. So rapid had been their advance that the town was evacuated in a panic; consequently little or no damage had been done to the buildings. From the military point of view Ramleh was indefensible, having no natural advantages. The enemy was wise in quitting a position which he had not a ghost's chance of holding.

As soon as the Aussies entered, they seized the large monastery which had been used for some time previous as the headquarters of the German aerial squadron. It had been left in the usual disgusting state, the result of Boche occupation. After it had been restored to a sanitary condition it was made into a hospital. It was admirably suited for a purpose which was not at all inconsistent with the design of its builders.

CHAPTER XXV

HOW THE WELSH TOOK BETHLEHEM, AND HOW JERU - SALEM FELL

PERHAPS no city in the world, whether ancient or modern, can outvie Jerusalem in the matter of site. Situated in the centre of the Judean highlands, at an elevation of some 2500 feet, it enjoyed through the circumjacent hills and intervening valleys a series of great natural defences. These, properly manned, rendered the Holy City well-nigh impregnable, except from attacks from the north. During the Roman occupation of Judea this weakness was provided against by the erection of a triple wall of great magnitude. The only way by which Jerusalem could be taken when properly defended, apart from treachery, was by starvation.

After expelling the Jebusites who inhabited this region, King David fixed upon the site for his royal habitation, because of the peculiar strength which it offered by its natural trenches and fortresses of valleys and hills. Built upon four hills—Moriah, Zion, Acra, and Bezetha—this most celebrated city in the whole world reared itself upon its lofty pinnacles in shining splendour.

It was this city that General Allenby's forces were now approaching and surrounding. What was impregnable in ancient times and in the Middle Ages, under the altered conditions of modern warfare may become so vulnerable as to give little trouble.

But before getting within striking distance of the enthroned city hard fighting and wise leadership were necessary. The British were now stretched from Nahr el Auja, a small river a few miles north of Joppa, on the left flank, in a south-easterly direction to Debir, the terminal point of the right flank; while an extended line held the western passes between.

It was Allenby's sound policy not to give the enemy breathing-time, and this meant, of course, no rest for the weary British. To add to the natural difficulties of the advance across the hill country, where obstacles were presented at every turn, the rains, which were long overdue, fell in a copious measure, swamping the lowlands, and making many of the mountain passes and tracks little less than quagmires. This added tremendously to the difficulties of transport.

Without doubt the ground advantages were with the enemy, both as regards the natural defences and the condition of the roads. The enemy's *morale*, it is true, had been weakened by his decisive defeats of the previous week; but, given a resolute command, there was still a favourable opportunity for rallying the broken battalions, rushing in reserves, and fighting the advance to a standstill. General Falkenhayn, high in the Kaiser's regard, to the discredit of his reputation made small use of his opportunity.

The Turks, it is true, rallied in certain parts, and offered a stubborn resistance: at Latron, for instance, on the Jaffa-Jerusalem line, where they put up a stiff fight; at Kirjath-jearim, too—a spot of peculiar interest to historians and to devout Jews, for it was here that the Ark of the Covenant was guarded for twenty years, after it had been given up by the Philistines, who had captured it, because of the bad luck it brought to them. Yet on the whole the enemy failed to make the most of his advantages.

The central attacking force was now striking hard blows and advancing slowly into the heart of the Judean hills. The whole character of the country was such that an invading army might easily meet with a total defeat by being hemmed in, with an enemy occupying all the commanding positions. The western defiles were particularly difficult. The sides were precipitous, and there were no roads save the torrent beds, consisting mostly of loose shingle. These, in the wet season, were converted into torrential streams; while the limestone strata, in roughly broken formation, made the passage of the defiles to be problems of a serious nature.

Nothing more need be said to convince the readers that the advance of the crusaders was anything but a picnic, and that it involved good generalship and indomitable resolution.

The road of the least resistance was that which from time immemorial has been famous. The Vale of Ajalon is a name to conjure with in Palestinian history. It was along this valley that the warrior Joshua met and overcame the stout resistance of the aboriginal tribes in his conquest of Canaan. Advancing from Jericho, he marched triumphantly to Gibeon and Gilgal. The Canaanites met him in great strength, but the old warrior was not to be denied. He routed them with heavy slaughter, and drove them along the way of the heights of Beth Horon to the sea, in headlong retreat and confusion. To make the day a long one in order that he might make the rout complete, he issued his famous challenge to the forces of Nature:

> "Sun; stand thou still upon Gibeon!
> And thou moon, in the valley of Ajalon!
> And the sun stood still, and the moon stayed.
> Until the people had avenged themselves upon their enemies.
> Is it not written in the book of Jasher?
> So the sun stood still in the midst of heaven.
> And hasted not to go down about a whole day."

It was by this route that the first crusaders reached Jerusalem. From a height along this way Samuel Mountjoy got his first enraptured view of the Holy City. History tells us that King Richard shut his eyes when he reached the commanding situation, and prayed that he might not see Zion until he could wrest it from the Saracens.

Pushing along this way, the main body of the British, the twentieth-century crusaders, at length reached the spot made memorable by Joshua's defeat of the Canaanites

—the pass of the Beth Herons of Biblical history, but known to moderns as Beit Ur el-Tahta and Beit Ur el-Foka. Could they seize and hold this strongly guarded pass they would be able to threaten the great northern highway, the Jerusalem-Nablus road.

The determined advance along the plains and into the heart of the hill country was now brought to a temporary standstill, as the attacking parties were far in advance of their supplies. Besides, it was necessary to make the lines of communication sure, and also to improve the roadway. The advance naturally could not be confined to the roads. The troops had to make many *détours*, and forge ahead through country devoid of roads, and which lent itself, every step of the way, to defensive tactics. While it was true that there was a lack of organisation and concerted action upon the part of the Turks, our advance was not undisputed. The enemy kept up an intermittent warfare, and their favourite sport of sniping found good opportunities in the hiding-places of the rocky uplands.

One of the problems to be solved was that of getting the guns into positions where they could act as a shield to the advance. The one fairly good road leading through the Vale of Ajalon had been mined in critical places by the retreating army, and had to be restored. This was accomplished with the utmost expedition. Meanwhile the Scots made a pathway over hills and gullies for a length of six miles, and then helped the gunners to handle the guns and bring them into effective position.

The British now made a strong attack upon the two Beth Herons, and particularly an overlooking ridge known as El Burj. Singular to say, El Burj is closely associated with Richard Coeur de Lion. He built a fortress there while on the same errand, to protect the very road along which a section of the British crusaders was advancing. Some crumbling remains of that fort still exist. Here the Turks put up a most determined resistance. On one occasion they counter-attacked, almost reaching the British trenches.

The southern point of the pass Beit Ur el-Foka was also

stoutly defended. As often as we took it we were obliged to evacuate it. So it changed hands several times, because it was dominated by other positions held by the Turks and the British respectively.

But while one section of the forces was so engaged, another turned its attention to a commanding hill farther to the south, bearing the modem name of Neby Samwil. This is the traditional tomb of Samuel, the great Hebrew prophet, the last of the judges of ancient Israel before it became a kingdom under King Saul. The capture of this strongly defended mountain was of the utmost value to us. All the violent attempts to dispossess us failed. An artillery attack, designed to blow us off the heights, while it failed in its object, did considerable damage to the sacred shrine, built upon the summit of the mountain, to commemorate Samuel's supposed resting-place.

Meanwhile, the aircraft were not idle. On one occasion five big German taubes fiercely attacked an equal number of British aeroplanes. It was a keen fight, watched by the troops of both sides in the vicinity. The result was a presage of our ultimate victory over the Moslem and the Boche. The taubes, after being worsted in the aerial encounter, beat a speedy retreat, one of their number being totally destroyed, while another was driven down out of control.

Holding Neby Samwil with a firm grasp, thus dominating the whole of the surrounding country, the British advance swept southward, seizing the beautiful village of Ain Karim. This picturesque place is associated with John the Baptist. Tradition has fixed it as the birthplace of the forerunner of Christ.

It has a modern interest in that it holds a community of Russian nuns. Here, in buildings nestling among groves of trees, the good women carry on the work pertaining to their Order. We now commanded a fine road leading from Ain Karim to Jerusalem.

Crossing the valley of Rephaim, still marching south, the railway line is struck at Bittir, the last station before entering Jerusalem. This ancient site, too, is replete with history, and is memorable for being the spot where the false Messiah, Bar Chockba, who rose in rebellion against Rome about the middle of the second century, was brought to book. He, and the fanatical Jews associated with him, fortified Bittir to withstand the Roman siege. They were, however, as water in the hands of their enemies. A fearful carnage ensued, in which the gutters of the streets ran with a torrent of blood.

But what has the right flank of the army been doing all this while?

While the central and left-flank forces were advancing through the hill country, as described, overcoming all the obstacles of travel, and capturing large numbers of the enemy as they progressed, the eastern units were carrying out the orders of the Chief of Staff.

And now the time had come to start their enveloping movement from the south. At the beginning of this operation they encountered but little opposition. They held the Hebron road, and advanced northward up the gradual ascent which led to the high country beyond. The region which the crusaders passed through presented many pleasing features. Like most places in Palestine it was cram-full of things having historical significance.

After leaving Dhahariyeh the road began to rise sharply. The remains of terraces all along the line, and particularly on the hillsides, showed plainly that in the olden times almost every foot of the land had been cultivated. In the present advance Arabs were frequently to be seen ploughing, sometimes with camels, at others with a yoke of oxen. The plough was practically the same as that used in ancient days when the Patriarchs wandered with their flocks and herds—a rude implement, having but one handle, and scratching the ground some two or three inches deep.

Apart from the snipers and small parties of scouts, the advance had little to contend against. The Wady Burghais was at length reached. The troops were now in a land of water-brooks and springs issuing from the limestone rocks. Noble olive trees grew in successive tiers up the sides of seemingly hopeless hills. Fertile valleys and plains were successively crossed. Another rough, sharp ascent, and the eager crusaders looked down upon the ancient and venerable city of Hebron.

Viewed thus from the distance it presented a beautiful appearance. It took the shape of a large, circular basin, formed by the surrounding hills. Lining the slopes of the hills were plantations of olive trees, and within the basin was a compact mass of grey limestone houses, with rounded domes. On the nearer edge lay a blue sheet of water, and up the hillside was the great and conspicuous Haram building, where rest the ashes of the Patriarchs. This, as an object of interest, overshadowed everything else.

Before long the troops were marching through the narrow and exceedingly dirty streets of Hebron, in undisputed possession. The curiously-minded were now able to examine the chief object of interest in the place. The Haram, a high, wide, windowless building of stone, covers the historic spot known as the Cave of Machpelah, the last resting-place of Abraham and Sarah; of Isaac and Rebecca; of Jacob and Leah. Rachel's Tomb is on the road midway between Bethlehem and Jerusalem.

It must not be forgotten that during the first seven years of David's reign Hebron was a royal city. Here he held court, and no doubt composed some of his immortal songs.

And now, while the central forces and those on the left wing keenly contested every disputed position, until at length they were in possession of every one of the western defences of Jerusalem, those to the south were advancing from Hebron, and soon reached Bethlehem and pushed up to the east of the Holy City.

To fully understand the nature of the final advance on the right flank, we must follow the fortunes of the Welsh;

for to the gallant men of the Principality was given the honour of carrying out an important piece of work. In this they received assistance from the Imperial Camelry.

The Welshmen had already won high praise. The task set them at the Gaza-Beersheba offensive was an extraordinarily difficult one. To capture the Kuweylfey Ridge was necessary to the success of our turning movement after the capture of Beersheba. It presented enormous difficulties of approach because of its precipitous character. The goat-like advance of the resolute Welsh up the crags and slopes was met by a rain of bombs from the heights above. Naught, however, could check the desperate valour of the attackers. Gaining a footing in the redoubt, they soon had the Turks at their mercy. The chagrined enemy, now strongly reinforced, attacked again and again from the north, where the approach was more accessible; but 'twas all in vain. The counter-attacks were stalled off in brilliant fashion.

The Welshmen were now in the van, advancing along the northern route. Pushing their way up through rain and slush, they neared Bethlehem. But though the advanced patrols had little difficulty in driving out the Turks, who at this stage seemed to have little stomach for fighting, they were not going to romp unhindered to the goal of their desires. Jacko put up a bit of a fight at Solomon's Pools, from which the Bethlehemites get their supply of water through an ancient aqueduct. He held a strong position here, and ought to have made things very bad for us. But, afraid of being outflanked by the menace on his right, he soon quitted, leaving the way open.

The same may be said of his tactics at Bethlehem. He had posted his field guns on the outskirts, and looked at one time as if he would require a lot of shifting. Opening with a heavy fire, he inflicted many casualties; but upon a flanking movement on the Welsh left which threatened his rear, he yielded to panic, and scuttled.

The Welsh entered Bethlehem at daybreak, and continued their advance to the north and north-east. Past

Rachel's Tomb, and along the valley of Rephaim they went, and then across Kedron; and very soon after they were facing the Mount of Olives a mile to the east of Jerusalem, from which it is separated by the Valley of Jehoshaphat.

As they look out on this high mount, heavily defended by the Turks, who are making here their last stand for the defence of Jerusalem, they become conscious that a vigorous attack is going on. The Londoners, who have come round from the west to the north, are in the act of advancing up the northern slopes in a bayonet charge. They are met by the desperate Turks, and a fierce duel ensues. Who will prevail? But the Welsh have no leisure moments for speculation.

Swinging into formation of attack, they cut in from the east on the Turk's flank, and completed his discomfiture. Those who can get away are flying down the Jericho road, leaving Jerusalem to her fate.

Even while the final volleys were being fired on the Mount of Olives, the white flag of surrender waved from the gateway of Jerusalem, and at eight o'clock on the morning of the 9th of December, 1917, the Mayor came out with a flag of truce and made full surrender to General Allenby's representative.

At this, the people, who had flocked into the streets and roadways, made a demonstration of welcome to their deliverers; while the women and girls, as on the day of our Saviour's public entry, scattered flowers and palm leaves on the way.

Jerusalem is ours!

CHAPTER XXVI

HOW THE PEOPLE OF JERUSALEM RECEIVED GENERAL ALLENBY

JERUSALEM, *December* 1917.
DEAR FAMILY,—You will already have received the cable from Jock, Tim, and myself. I guess both you and the Mackenzies were a little bit pleased when you knew that we had come through all right.

"I hope you good people noted the above address at the first glance. Jerusalem! Yes. I am actually writing this letter from a Jerusalem café. It is a truly cosmopolitan place: Greeks, Italians, Austrians and French seem all mixed up in the business. But before I say anything about the city, I will say one or two things about the happenings of last week or so.

"I may as well begin by saying that I got a nasty spill during the stunt; but before that, I managed to get a clip with a bit of shell on the thigh. That was at the taking of Beersheba. This had got pretty right when I had the misfortune to come a cropper through my nag putting his foot on a loose stone as we were rushing a nest of Turks, who were ensconced among some boulders on the high side of a rocky hill. The men thought at first that I had stopped one. They were carrying me back when I came to, for I'd been knocked a bit dilly. I made them put me down as soon as I knew what was happening, and go back to their mates, who were nosing out the Jackoes. They would only do this on the assurance that I carried no lead, and that it was a simple case of spill. By good luck, who should come along at that moment but old Hogan. He was following up with the field ambulance. There's no doubt about it, Tim's my good genius. You should have seen the face of the 'Junior Partner of the Amalgamateds' when he spotted me lying on the roadside at the foot of the hill! I suppose my face was white, and I was shikkered with the bump. One would have thought I was a dying baby. In fact it was Tim's fiddle face and Irish lament, as he bent over me, that tonicked me up. You should have seen his petrified look and glaring eyeballs as my machine-gun, fully loaded with my vocabulary of British and foreign expletives, rattled its contents over him!

"To make a long story short, the dear old rascal soon had my side and arm, which were considerably bruised, painted over with iodine and bandaged up. After a little while I was able to get into the saddle, and follow up. My men—I was leading a troop at the time—had by this time done their work, capturing those whom they did not knock over, and suffering but few casualties during the operation.

"I have been in some very interesting places during the stunt. I was at the taking of Jaffa. There are a number of Jews there, mostly in the business line. My word! the poor beggars have had a time of it from the Turks and the Germans since the war started. All the leading Jews were arrested and charged with espionage. The trial was a farce. They were convicted on trumped-up evidence, and publicly hanged in the presence of their wives and children. I spoke to several of the wives and children who have been so horribly bereaved. It was a pitiful sight. By George! the wretches richly deserve to be paid back in their own coin with compound interest! One feels mad enough to do anything in the way of reprisal when he comes across such cases as these.

"I don't think, mind you, that the Turks would be so vindictive if they were not put up to it by the Germans. *They're* the dizzy limit for dishonour and cruelty. They befoul every symbol of decency and honour. Here's an incident. It took place during the stunt, and is typical. One of the advancing battalions—the Scots, I think—were rooting out a nest of machine-guns. They put up a box barrage round the position, and made it so hot for the Turks that they stuck up the white flag. This was held up by the German officer who was in command. At this, one of our officers approached to question him. When this man was a few paces away the execrable Boche pulled out a revolver, which he had hidden, shot the unsuspecting officer dead, and then bolted. He almost got away, too. However, he was captured, after a sharp sprint, by a Kiltie. There is no need for me to say anything further about him. You will guess at first pop what ensued. The misery of it is, that this particular man is a type that abounds in the German army.

"Here is another incident of a different character, and one which concerns myself. After the capture of Jaffa, my regiment, in conjunction with others, moved to the north-east. We were making for the river Auja, where we were to occupy a position which would make it easier for the main body to advance towards Jerusalem. Just south of the wady we captured a body of Turks—bagged the whole lot without a casualty on our part. The ease with which we did this was largely due to the fact that they were in a parlous condition. Among them were two officers. You may judge of my surprise when I found in one of them the captain who commanded the cavalry patrol which collared M'Thirst and myself while we were legging it from the Bedouins. It was Jock M'Thirst, by the way, who first identified this chap when he was conducting the two men to me.

"I knew the captain as soon as I sighted him, though the recognition was not mutual. That, perhaps, was not to be wondered at very much. The poor fellow was in a sorry plight. It seems he had been wounded during the Gaza bombardment, and showed real pluck in sticking to it in the way he did. He and his men were on the verge of starvation. Taken altogether, they were a dispirited and sick-looking crowd. I, too, must have cut a pretty queer figure. I certainly would have been out of place in a drawing-room. My tunic was proudly carrying many battle scars, while what with smoke and dust I had a pretty thick coating of muck on my face. Under these circumstances there was little to wonder at the Turk not recognising me.

"I soon enlightened him, however; and you should have seen the expression on his face as he realised how completely the tables had been turned. Mortification and chagrin chased each other over his dirty face as he stared at me.

"'Look here, Captain,' said I, 'it's the fortune of war: me yesterday, you to-day. I can sympathise with you, but don't be downhearted. You've got the same sporting chance as I had, when you nabbed us, of doing a skip. Meanwhile, for the sake of old times, I'll make you as comfortable as circumstances permit; though, of course, I cannot, under the present conditions, put you up as royally as you did me in your Headquarters.'

"'That was a dastardly return you made for the hospitality shown you, by stealing our plans!' cried he, with some heat, despite his forlorn condition, as soon as I mentioned Headquarters.

"'Not at all,' replied I. 'I was not there as your guest. I was a prisoner, and refused parole. As much a prisoner as though you had immured me in a dungeon. I was not only a prisoner: I was an enemy. We were at war. However criminal my actions would have been under other conditions, the present circumstances justified the theft. When the opportunity presented itself of getting information regarding your positions and men, it was my clear duty as an enemy to secure it, even though I had to purloin it. If, on the other hand, you had caught me with the plans you would have been quite justified in ending my career with an unfriendly bullet. I knew the risk I was taking. Look here, old man, wouldn't you have done the same had you been in my place? Yes, and gloried in it. You know jolly well you would.'

"He couldn't deny it, of course. Before long, however, I worked him into a cheerful mood, and as we trotted along to our camp I questioned him as to the motive underlying his general's treatment of M'Thirst and myself, when we fell into their hands. It has always been a puzzle to me, and still is. His explanation didn't let much daylight in. It was to the effect that the Turks were greatly puzzled over our strategy, and the general, it appears, was hoping to squeeze me. Hence his pose of friendliness, and the extra-good treatment that Jock and I got from him. That's all very well. But somehow or other I don't feel satisfied that it is the true explanation. There was another motive, I feel sure.

"As far as one can judge from outward signs, the Jerusalemites are devoutly thankful for our victory. Many of the Turkish civilians, even, profess to be pleased at the change of masters. No wonder! A large number of the inhabitants are existing, not living, on the verge of starvation. Lots have died of hunger and disease. They are convinced that the British will see to it that they have ample food. You may bet they will. Talk about beggars! I thought we'd seen all there was to see of the art in Egypt, but the Gyppoes can't hold a candle to the fraternity here. They have brought deception to the point of a fine art. Why, some of the young girls I've seen practising it here would take in their own parents.

"We found out after our occupation that the Turks and Germans were astounded beyond measure at our successes at Beersheba and Gaza. Enver Pasha, it seems, reached here last month, just after Beersheba had fallen, and got as far south as Hebron, in company with General von Falkenhayn. It was there that the decision was made to defend Jerusalem. To help in these defensive measures a number of German officers were added to the army, in order to stiffen the resistance. Yet, despite all their planning, Jerusalem is ours, never again to pass into Moslem hands.

"Now, a word about General Allenby's official and public entry. It was not anything like what was expected. There was little or no flourishing of trumpets. Twenty years or so ago, if you remember, the Kaiser did Palestine: he made the Grand Tour as the Protector of the Mohammedans, and no doubt had a regular royal time. He had a portion of the walls knocked down to make a wide entry. And didn't he enter in style! All the pomp and trappings of State and Militarism surrounded his august person. What a significant contrast to the business-like entry of our general! No walls were razed to the ground, but the Jaffa Gate, rarely opened, was used for entrance. This iron gate is called by the Arabs by a name which means, 'the friend.' Could anything have been more within the fitness of things? Depend upon it, the Jerusalemites know by this time who are their real friends. One thing is absolutely certain, they have no time for the Hun, and are quite disillusioned about the pretentious Kaiser.

"Well, I suppose our war correspondents have telegraphed a graphic account of it to the papers. What Massey misses in the way of copy isn't worth having. Simple as the march in was, it was wonderfully effective, and will be remembered long after the Kaiser's theatrical display has been relegated to the limbo of melodramatic vanities. When it became known that the entrance would be made through the Jaffa Gate, the road thereto was crowded by pedestrians of all classes and nationalities, who had come out of the city to hail the conqueror. They were all in holiday costume. It was a thrilling sight to view the oncoming of the populace. This was heightened as our *cortége* passed through the Jaffa Gate and along the picturesque if evil-smelling streets. Those who hadn't come out were on the flat-topped roofs of the houses.

And, my, didn't they raise a shindy! Tongues in many languages were acclaiming under high pressure.

"Sir Edmund entered on foot. He was accompanied by a small guard which was thoroughly representative of the dominions of the Empire. In addition were some Italian and French soldiers. It was my wonderful luck to be one of the Aussies who took part in the march. I think I hear Ella saying, 'Jack's got a swelled head.' If I haven't, Ella, it'll be a hit of a surprise. I'm very human, you know.

"Well, to continue: Previous to entering, the military governor received General Allenby, and conducted him along the prescribed route. On our general's right was the French commander, and on his left, the Italian. In addition to the Guard of Honour, composed of English, Irish, Scotch, Welsh, Australians, New Zealanders, and Indians, were several *attaches*, and members of the General Staff. The procession, which advanced to Mount Zion, stopped at the steps by which David's Tower is approached. At this stage the proceedings became severely official. A proclamation was made in four languages, setting forth that civil and religious freedom would be guaranteed, and that every religious building and shrine would be respected and protected. Further, that no act of injustice would be allowed to pass without adequate punishment. The procession then moved on to a large open square where our general received the big bugs of the city, including the heads of the religious denominations, whose names, by the way, is legion. Then came the civic fathers and other notabilities. Many of the religious heads, who had been forced to leave by the Turks, were there by deputy.

"When the circuit of the city was made, the *cortége* returned to the Jaffa Gate. In order to show how careful General Allenby is not to wound the religious susceptibilities of the people, the Temple area was put under a military cordon, composed of Indian Moslem soldiers. A selected officer has been appointed to look after all the Holy Places.

"At present I am here in charge of a military guard, but expect to be soon relieved, as the Light Horse are still on the go along the Jericho road.

"I can write no more this time. Good-bye. With love, yours   ever,

JACK."

"P.S.—I quite forgot to say that through the promotion of my colonel, I've got his billet as colonel, with brevet rank; and old Mackenzie's got mine. What price that, Ella? I mean Mac's promotion.—J. S."

THE END